Tiddler to Ripe

a story from school benches to college garden

Hitesh Santwani

©Hitesh Santwani 2021

All rights reserved

All rights reserved by author. No part of this publication may be reproduced, stored in a retrieval system or transmitted in any form or by any means, electronic, mechanical, photocopying, recording or otherwise, without the prior permission of the author.

Although every precaution has been taken to verify the accuracy of the information contained herein, the author and publisher assume no responsibility for any errors or omissions. No liability is assumed for damages that may result from the use of information contained within.

First Published in May 2021

ISBN: 978-93-5427-557-9

BLUEROSE PUBLISHERS
www.bluerosepublishers.com
info@bluerosepublishers.com
+91 8882 898 898

Cover Design:
Joshua Freitas

Typographic Design:
Namrata Saini

Distributed by: BlueRose, Amazon, Flipkart, Shopclues

Acknowledgment

I am really thankful to my dearest family and friends, and God. Last but not least no matter how much I thank them, it won't be worth it because they deserve more than a word of thanks, and they are MY STUDENTS. Yes, it is true that students are generally inspired by their teachers; but in the current generation, I am very lucky to have such students in my life, who are always a motivation to others irrespective of whether the person in front of them is a teacher, an elder, a younger person, or a complete stranger. I would also like to express my deep gratitude towards BlueRosePublishers and their entire team.

Contents

Chapter One: The Sleepover 1

Chapter Two: Malav's Childhood Diary 6

Chapter Three: Three Angels 16

Chapter Four: Manish's Entry in My Life................ 38

Chapter Five: The Beginning of College Life 53

Chapter Six: Sweet Moments................................... 74

Chapter Seven: Roman 101

Chapter Eight: True Love Won 115

Chapter Nine: Valentine Shocks 125

Chapter Ten: The Entry of a Villain........................ 157

Chapter Eleven: The Result of Waiting for
True Love 177

Chapter Twelve: Unanswered Questions................ 195

Author's Note 198

CHAPTER ONE

The Sleepover

'Circumstances play a great role in our life, isn't it?' I asked my best friend Prakash. I replied in the affirmative and noticed him musing, so I asked if there was any problem. Since Prakash was my best friend, I could tell something was wrong and more so I had been observing such facial expressions since he recently returned from Madhya Pradesh (MP). 'Hitesh', he said, 'Do you remember who my best friend was before I met you?'

I replied, 'Obviously, my Alter Ego, your only friend in MP, Malav!'

He smiled. 'So, you met him this time and now you are missing him?'

Just for lifting his mood, I added, 'Hey, please don't say that you have changed your taste. Do you like him now instead?'

But he replied angrily, 'Yes, I even had sex with him. Are you jealous of him?' I laughed, 'No, not at all.'

'Stop kidding Hitesh, I am serious.' My laughter subsided sensing his graveness and suddenly I saw his eyes brimming with tears.

'Hey Praku, so sorry, but now you are going to tell me everything, what is the matter?' He wiped his tears and said, 'When I went to Malav's home, it was locked; so I asked his neighbours about his whereabouts and they informed me that he and his family had left that place 2 years ago, so I decided to call him up but his number didn't exist. I asked everyone for his new address, but nobody knew about it, except for an elderly woman who informed me that an incident had happened in their home, so they shifted to Delhi.

So I was left with no hope to meet him in the future, but the next day I again went there and came to know that the house they lived in still belongs to them only, so I decided to break in in the hope of finding a clue to his whereabouts. So, I entered inside his house by breaking a window of the drawing room. The house was fully covered with white sheets and there was a lot of dust everywhere. I went straight towards Malav's room and opened his cupboard. I found an old school bag but as soon as I took out the bag, one blank white paper and one peacock feather fell from it. So, I bent down to pick that paper and turned it around.' The ring of a phone interrupted our conversation, and it was a call from my home to Praku's cell phone. Oh shit, I didn't know where the hell my phone was which meant that mom would be worried for me. I picked up the call, and before I could say anything, mom was scolding me for my carelessness.

Praku found my cell phone and handed it over to me. I saw there were 17 missed calls from home. I apologised to mom and she slowly calmed down. She asked when I would be back as it was already quarter past ten, and my home is far from Praku's home, so I replied, 'Mom, I am not coming tonight, I want to catch up with Praku, as he has returned after such a long time.' Mom agreed and Praku passed me a smile.

Then we decided to spend the night at his terrace so no-one could disturb us. So we informed his mother and we started to walk towards the stairs, but I paused and he turned towards me and asked, 'What?'

I replied very politely, 'My friend, who will take that bag which you have brought from MP?'

He answered, 'Who told you that I have brought the bag?'

I replied, 'My friend, I am damn sure you have brought it, and your emotions are attached to its very fabric. I know you very well.' He smiled and went inside his room; he came back with the bag and then we settled on the terrace under one small light bulb and continued our conversation. I reminded him that we were discussing the paper fallen from Malav's cupboard.

He continued, 'Oh. Yes, when I turned the paper, there was a picture of a girl. A cute girl with an elegant smile and her hairs straight open dressed in blue coloured saree with red zari work on its border with a red coloured necklace and earrings. She was looking incredibly beautiful. If I am not wrong that picture could be of traditional day or some similar occasion. But she was looking fantastic and attractive.'

I asked, 'But who was she?' He replied, 'I don't know. She might be his girlfriend, his friend, his cousin or just a picture from the Internet. He is the only son of his parents, so she can't be his sister.'

I asked, 'Okay, then what was in the bag?'

He answered, 'Something related to your hobby. Any guesses?'

I thought for a moment, and then I thought that he is like me and shouted excitedly, 'A diary?!'

He gave me a cute smile. I took the bag from his hand, but he didn't give it to me and said, 'I will allow you to read his diary only on one condition.'

I asked, 'And what would that be?'

He said, 'If you promise me to help me find his whereabouts. Besides you are a good writer so I want you to write a novel on his story.' I promised him and at present, I am fulfilling it. He passed me the bag and I took out his diary from the bag.

I said, 'But before I start reading this, I have one question in my mind.' He nodded his head. I asked, 'If I am not wrong, Malav is not a Sindhi name, but you are telling his caste is the same as ours, how's that possible?'

After I completed what I had to say, he had a strange smile on his face. He started, 'During his childhood, everyone used to tease Malav with the same question, sometimes even he got angry on everyone and shouted on his parents also, but his parents could never answer him to his satisfaction. But I still remember when I was coming to Surat, his Dad was talking with me and during our conversation, I asked the same question to his dad, Shankar Patwani. At that time Malav was not near us, so he answered my question. He informed me that his best friend had the same name and when Malav's mother, Asha Patwani, was pregnant with him, his best friend had passed away in a car accident in an attempt to save Malav and Asha Aunty. So, as a mark of respect, he gave that name to Malav. Moreover, Malav even has very similar features with him. But Asha Aunty was frightened to share this with Malav because he is a very sensitive person and he might start thinking that one person had given up his life in order to save him. So Uncle and Aunty decided not to tell him about this matter. I respect him for his decision'. I replied, 'Okay, so this is the reason behind his name. Anyways, now shall we start reading his diary?' He replied in the affirmative and I opened his diary.

CHAPTER TWO

Malav's Childhood Diary

'Dear Diary. I am Malav Patwani and today I am writing to you for the very first time. I have completed my SSC just last month and currently my vacations are going on and I am making the most of them by watching with TV and playing cricket for almost the whole day. But today I am feeling a bit low because my bestie, Prakash, is going to shift to Surat permanently and I am going to miss him a lot. This is one of the reasons I started writing this diary. At the same time, I am happy about our decision of giving 'goodnight missed calls' to each other every night before sleeping. He is leaving day after tomorrow and I hope that before going, he writes something about me in my diary. I will ask him to do so tomorrow.'

'How cutely he had written, this shows he was an innocent child!' I said.

Praku smiled and said, 'Please don't comment in between, or else we will be unable to get his story and his feelings.' I promised not to talk until we complete reading. And similarly, from now on I am writing as Malav for you all.

Finally, I convinced Prakash to write something for me.

Hello, I am Prakash Kotak. Yes, unfortunately, due to my father's transfer, I am going to Surat permanently, and like Malav, I am going to miss him a lot. I don't know where our life will take us, but I really wish that in the future we get a chance to live together in one city. Now as per my best friend's wish, I am going to write about him.

M - Mastermind

A - Attractive

L - Lovely

A - Amazing

V - Victorious

None of the above qualities are present in him. He is a very simple, innocent, and an emotional boy. Though he is not a narrow-minded person, still he is frightened to talk to girls, even in this generation. He is very shy. He secretly liked 3 girls in our class, but when I asked him what he had seen in them, he replied that they are toppers. Oh My God! What would happen to him, I don't know. Anyway, except this, he is a very frank, helpful and a pure hearted person. He respects elders. I am glad to write this that unlike the present generation of boys he can live without using abusive words. And his golden words whenever anyone asks him about his lifestyle are, 'My parents already taught me and made me feel about the importance of responsibilities, good, evil, money, and relations, hence whatever I am, I am happy.' These words always touch my heart. And yes, I know his world's biggest happiness is in his father's hands. He becomes very happy whenever he listens to good words for himself from his father's mouth. He always does what his dad was doing. Sometimes I feel he does not deserve to be born in this generation, *because he doesn't even like pizzas, burgers, and any junk food except Pav Bhaji. Even his mother used to call him 'Gandhi Bapu' while referring to his eating habits. His favourite dish is dal and rice. And yes, the most interesting quality about him which attracts everyone towards him is that even if he becomes someone's casual friend then surely within two days, that person would want to become his close friend. He is too frank and trusts everyone very easily. Sometimes he can show such great understanding which even elders are not able to show. I have such a good understanding of him because I knew about his two secret aims. His first aim is as I wrote, to hear good words from his dad for himself. And his second aim in life is to avoid creating a generation gap and always trying to maintain every relationship and matter in such a way that people of both generations are satisfied, happy, and together. I respect him a lot. Though he is not able to fulfil his second aim all the time, but still he has a great and special space in my heart and life because I have never seen anyone with such high aims. I am lucky to have such a best friend. Thanks a ton Malav for always being present in my life.*

Your childhood buddy,

Prakash S. Kotak

Oh, I am glad to know about all this. I am so happy that at least there is one person in my life who understands me in every possible way. Thanks, a lot, to you too Prakash and thanks a lot to God also. I am going to miss you very much Prakash.

Finally, I along with our common friend Pradeep dropped Praku and his family at the station and he started a journey for his new life. May God bless him! Pradeep was a quiet and studious child, but he was my friend before I met Prakash. Anyway we both were going to miss him a lot. Finally, my SSC results were out and I opted for the science stream for my further studies, even Pradeep chose the same, so we took admission in the same school and went to the same classes for IIT coaching.

In our coaching classes initially we were enrolled in the MP Board, but as we both were good in studies so sir shifted us in Central Board Batch. I was very happy to hear these words, but when I attended the CBSE Batch, I was shocked as soon as I saw the classroom atmosphere. Till tenth grade, we had never talked to any girls, but here some boys and girls were sitting together, some were chatting on their cell phones, some were fighting, and doing all sorts of activities together though everyone became serious when sir started to teach.

Here the teaching was also a little bit different since along with studies, sir loved to have fun and to make jokes, so studies were not boring for me now. I started liking this atmosphere, but Pradeep was not liking all it at all. I thought this new atmosphere will surely change my life a lot and may even be a turning point in my life.

Over time, I changed, but Pradeep remained the same. I even started talking to girls, and within a few days, I almost knew everyone after I topped one class test. Even class topper Vicky became a good friend of mine now and I entered in his group, though it was not planned, it was just happening in my life and I was following what I felt right at that moment. When I entered that group of toppers, I started to change myself; if anyone called me anytime; I was always ready to go with them. I liked them so much that I always accepted whatever they said. I accepted their decency and their standards, without thinking whether it's right for me or not, whether I liked them or not, I was just blindly following them. We were only in grade eleven and still we had some couples in our batch. As I was slowly accepting this atmosphere, I was feeling the absence of a partner in my life. Though Pradeep was still at the same place, I think now I had walked ahead in my life. So, now Pradeep talked to me only when he had some work with me, or when I had some work with him. Then the entry of three girls in the class changed my life. The very first girl Arti entered at the end of grade eleven. She had shifted from Bihar, and on the very first day of her class she sat on the first bench with her sister, Princess, and I was sitting on the second bench. I saw her and she turned her face towards me, and she passed me a smile, and in response, I did the same. But from inside, I was flying on cloud nine as a girl had smiled at me for the very first time. While returning from the class, I was too happy with her smile and I was with Pradeep, so I laid a bet with him that she would talk with me surely the next day and I won the bet. On the very next day, she talked to me. I still remember her first words to me.

'Are you Malav?' she asked, and I replied in the affirmative.

She said, 'I don't know, but some boy had hacked my Orkut account and he had the same name.'

'But I am not that boy.'

'Yes, I know. Don't worry, I am not blaming you, I am just informing you. By the way, my name is Arti.' With these words, she put her hand forward. My feelings were undetectable, but the first time I shook hands with any girl. Though formal, I loved that moment. Then suddenly I came to know that the management faculties of our classes had resigned from our institute and two new teachers were appointed in place of them. Those two teachers are the other two girls of my life who changed my life.

They both contributed immensely in my life. The first girl was Priya Ma'am, who was also Sindhi and even was my distant family relative, so I used to call her Priya di. After a few days, her friend named Kruti ma'am joined our classes. On the very first day, Priya di recognised me, but I didn't as I had seen her when I was very small. She was only five years older than me. On the second day, when sir sent Pradeep and me outside for paying our fees, we had to talk to Priya di as she was the management faculty. She asked the final date for the payment of fees, and we gave it. But I felt happy because she was talking with me in Sindhi, gave me a very sweet smile, and allowed us to go inside classroom, but before going in I realised and I just turned my face towards her, and she nodded and said, 'I am one about whom you are thinking.'

I was feeling very happy to see her and she understood what was going on in my mind. But as the class was going on, so she instructed me to go in. After the class, I went to meet her. I was so excited, as it was the same day on which I was born. And God had given me the best gift by bringing her in my life on that lucky day. She wished me, and I bought chocolate for her and Kruti ma'am and even took blessings of both as both were my guide. When I started my vehicle, Arti called me, and she came towards me and gave me the statue of Lord Ganesha as a birthday present which she had made by her hand with sand. First, it shocked me that we have talked only once, but then I accepted it and gave her a chocolate. But she said, 'Only a chocolate would not work, you have to give a party also.'

'Sure, but some other time as I am running late.' She smiled but I already knew that she wanted to be my friend. Anyways I was so happy as it was my best birthday ever, met with Priya di, Arti's Friendship, all thanks to Almighty. Slowly I started chatting with Arti on Orkut and soon I asked for her contact number, but she refused by informing me that she did not have a cell phone. But on the next day, she gave me the contact number of her sister and told me that we could chat on that number. Slowly our chats increased and so did our friendship. Now it was the time that made me feels too happy because my whole group was teasing me with her, though I was not in love. I felt very happy when Vicky or anyone from our group teased me with her (or with any other girl for that matter).

I still remember that one incident after which I started to believe in her imagination. Arti always used to say that she can talk to Lord Ganesha, so for teasing her, in response, I used to tell her that I can talk with Lord Krishna.

Though she knew that I didn't believe her, once she said, 'I can listen to his voice, because I love him, and even he loves me. Not always does he talk to me in a real voice, but sometimes either he passes me a message or response in such a way that if normal person notices then he or she may think it has just accidentally happened due to situations.' Once I went for a breakfast party with my friends during the break, so I invited Arti to join us.

Though she was fasting, she accompanied us just because I wanted to. While taking breakfast, suddenly she took out a new statue of Lord Ganesha and showed it to everyone. First, I felt weird because she had never shown it to me. Anyway, she might have forgotten. One-by-one, Arbaz, Rittzi, Vinod, and I saw it, and then continued our mischief. After completing our break, when we were going back to class, Arbaz asked me for my cell phone to call his sister as his mobile's battery was low. So, I gave him my phone and finally I got a chance to talk with Arti alone.

So I asked her, 'Why didn't you show that new statue first to me?'

She replied, 'Because you don't believe me that I talked to Ganesh Ji and I showed it to everyone because I felt he was telling me to do that, so I did that. And my dear friend, don't be possessive, no-one has dared to take your place in my life, you will always remain my first friend.' After completing her sentence, she already brought a smile on my face. Arbaz came back and handed me my phone back and then we headed to our classes.

Along with Arbaz and Vinod, I used to sit on the first bench, Arti and her sister used to sit on the second bench. And sometimes, in between class, Arti and I used to play with our legs, she always used to hit me with her leg, and I used to catch her leg, in between my legs. Once by mistake, instead of me, she hit her leg to Arbaz, and that idiot guy shouted. Arti said sorry to him, but he teased me by saying, '*Beta, teri wajay se muje padh rahi hai.*(Instead of you, I am beaten by her.)'

I tried to lower his voice but before I could do that sir caught us and asked us, and Arbaz told everything to sir that I and Arti were playing with our legs and everyone laughed including sir. Arbaz and Vinod were teasing me, I was feeling shy, and Arti was giving confused expressions and I couldn't fathom whether she was feeling shy, bad, happy, funny, or what.

The last lecture was conducted by our maths teacher so Arti went home as she had opted for biology instead of maths. Finally, classes were over and before going back home, I sat for ten minutes with Priya di.

Suddenly I was surprised to read Arti's text as she wrote, 'Jaanu, what are you doing?' Actually, *Mere mann me to laddu futa* (I was feeling ecstatic), so I decided to flirt, but I noticed that Priya di was watching me, so I kept my cell phone in my pocket without replying.

After five minutes, I came out and as soon as I was going to reply, Arbaz's call came, I was confused as I thought his cell phone had low battery, and in the short time which had elapsed he couldn't possibly have reached home so how could he have called. Anyway, there was no time to think as it was better to receive a call before it ended for saving balance, so I received and it gave me another shock when on another side it was Arti.

I didn't understand what was happening, but Arti on the other side said, 'My statue of Ganesha might have fallen somewhere in that breakfast shop. Can you please just go and check it? It's a request.'

I replied, 'Of course, but first tell me where you met Arbaz, and where is your Di's phone?'

But she shouted, 'First go and check it fast before it gets lost.' Oh My God, Arti loves Ganesha a lot, so I went, and found it on the floor where we were present, so I took it and kept it in my bag. So, I decided to call back, but I was unsure about the number to call on. Arbaz was still waiting for her.

But then suddenly the whole matter struck my mind that when Arbaz asked for my phone, he changed his number with Arti's. So, it was his message not Arti's. Thank God I didn't reply else Arti would have thought of me as the most flirty boy in class, and that idiot Arbaz would have told everything to everyone, and even everyone would have got to know that I like Arti. Slowly, I noticed that Arti was right, if her Ganesha had not told her to show the statue to everyone, it may not have fallen, and she might have not called me, I would have replied to Arbaz in place of Arti, and then in front of whole class I would have been embarrassed. Seriously Ganesha saved me. Finally, I started to believe her that she could talk to Ganesha.

Then I called her and informed her about the whole thing, she got little angry, but she said, 'He is your friend, so please handle him, and tell him to stay in his limits else if I get hurt, no-one can dare to do anything in front of me, once I get angry.'

I replied, 'Ok, you don't worry, I will handle him. Anyway, whatever happens always happens for good and from now on I believe in you and your imagination Arti.' She smiled. That night we had a long chat about Lord Ganesha.

CHAPTER THREE

Three Angels

Day by day, my chats with Arti were increasing, and I was feeling that we were getting closer to each other as she was my first female friend and maybe it was her wish to be my friend. I didn't prefer to be too close to girls. But I didn't get to know when Arti changed me and my rules. When I went to Pune for my cousin's wedding, I continued to chat with her. As she was the first girl in my life, so it was obvious that thoughts of 'I may like her or love her, or maybe she.....' popped up in my mind quite frequently. While in the family get together, I came to know that in our caste, the marriage was possible only if both partners belonged to the same caste. So suddenly I thought that if she loves me and if I started to love her too, then I won't be able to live without her, but as she is not a Sindhi, so I won't be able to marry her, because I can't marry someone, due to whom my parents get hurt. So, it was a dead end as far as I was concerned.

From that moment, I decided to maintain distance from her. I even replied to one of her messages saying, 'Please give me some space Arti. I want to spend some time with my girlfriend Neha.' I lied to her.

Initially she felt happy, then felt sad because she complained that I had hidden such a big matter from her. My doubt was a little bit converted to a belief that she loved me. But then she replied, 'I am happy that you have fallen in love. May Ganesha make you both one in the future!!'

I asked her, 'Have you ever fallen in love?' She replied, 'Idiot, every day I tell you that I love Ganesha and I am going to marry him only. By the way, where are you right now?'

I replied to her, 'I am watching a movie with her though I was at a movie with my cousins. But how will he marry you? He is not a human being, he is GOD.'

She replied, 'I know dear, but I don't have to worry about that. I believe in myself and even in him that either he will send someone for me or he will come for me as a human being himself. I just need to identify him that I can easily do, with his help only. I love him a lot. Anyways now you enjoy with her, and take some space from me, and will continue once you will be back. Bye. Take care.'

When I came back from Pune, I already prepared myself to lie to Arti even if she felt bad to lose me. I felt that she might be able to take it at this stage, but may not be able to do so in the future. I didn't want to hurt her, and I didn't want to hurt my parents ever. But when I entered the class and saw her, I was shocked. When she saw me, she passed me a very big smile and it was clear how happy she was for me!

If I was a girl or she was a boy, she would have hugged me till now. Priya Di and Kruti ma'am noticed her face and hence asked her the reason for her happiness, and she informed them about my new virtual girlfriend Neha.

Priya Di turned towards me, and I passed her a fake smile. She said, 'She seems happier than you.' I pointed towards Arti added, 'Control my friend, and be happy when I marry her.'

She replied, 'Don't worry Malu, You would surely marry her. I will talk to Ganesha for you.' Initially, I thought she was acting, but as days were passing, I realised that she was actually happy. I felt guilty as I had been thinking wrong things all this while. I thought she was attracted to me, but it was me, who was actually getting attracted towards her. It was me, who had thought like she was the first girl for me I would be the first for her too, but I was not the first boy in her life it seemed now. I thought she was immature, but again it was me. But now what else could I have done, as I had already lied. And as everybody knows, for keeping one lie, we have to tell several more lies. I was confused. At the end of the day, she asked me for the pending party. I gave her a chocolate, and told her, 'Party next time.'

Finally, she went back and even I was going back home, but Priya Di called me, and asked me, 'Why do you do this?'

With confused expressions, I asked her, 'Di, what have I done? What are you trying to say?'

She replied, 'I know you are lying about your girlfriend.' I responded to her with shocked expressions. She added, 'Dear, I have seen more Diwalis than you, I am more experienced than you!'

I replied to her, 'Didi, You know that inter-caste marriage is not allowed in our family. I was afraid that she will slowly become more attached towards me and so would I. If any one or both of us fall in love what would happen in the future! I neither want to hurt her nor my parents! But now I feel I was overthinking.'

She asked me, 'Is she your first female friend?' I nodded.

She said, 'Oh don't worry, it happens, when a person of the opposite sex becomes our friend for the first time. But yes, I am impressed by your intentions. I am feeling good to know that my student is a pure hearted person. Even though you are so small, you care for your parents, and you respect them as well. Besides them, you respect your friends too. So, my boy, *Ache logo ke saath kabhi galat nahi hota* (bad things never happen with good people). Go and tell her the truth, Arti will surely understand.'

I touched her feet, and she blessed me. I came home and was feeling good after talking with Priya Di. Later in the evening, I started chatting with Arti, and while chatting I showed the guts and told her everything truthfully. Within a second she forgave me, she understood that whatever I did was not due to any wrong intentions and even she liked my guts for confessing to her. I thanked God for giving me such an understanding friend. Now, I believed in the philosophy: '*Jo hota hai ache ke liye hota hai* [Whatever happens, always happens for the good].' Even after making such a huge mistake, day by day the mutual understanding between us increased, and so did our friendship. Now, we were clear about our aims, at least in our relationship status, but I always panicked, as I know love couldn't be planned, it just happened. I never ate yogurt earlier but once at a party when she offered it to me with her own hands and I didn't stop myself from eating it. She really had become my best friend.

For some days, Arti went to her hometown, Bihar and I was feeling her absence. And even Priya Di was also not coming to classes since the last few days. Sometimes only I and Kruti ma'am were together. One day after classes, we sat together for some time. She asked me, 'What's your relationship status with Arti?'

I replied to her, '*I Luv her.*' She replied with excitement, 'I knew that.' I interrupted and took a pen and book, and wrote, 'I Luv Arti but not Love.' She read and gave me confused expressions.

I explained to her, 'This is my theory: when the relationship between a boy and girl increases from friendship, but not as much that they are ready to commit for life then that unknown relation is named as 'Luv' by me. Ma'am, the world has not named such a relation, so I named it by myself for myself. It looks like love, but it spells different but still, no-one deeply knows the difference, so the word is almost the same, but a little bit different!'

She laughed and replied, 'Good thinking. You are young but are able to think a lot. Good, Good, I am impressed.'

I asked her about Priya di. She informed me that Priya di had met with an accident two days ago. After hearing this, I was shocked and asked her, 'What? How did this happen? And how is she?'

She replied, 'Calm Down, Malav. Her vehicle slipped. She is fine, but her right leg got fractured, so she is on complete bed rest for 21 days.'

I replied, 'Yes, I know when a fracture happens, one needs complete bed rest for 21 days. My right hand got fractured when I was in grade nine. But why didn't she inform me? Anyway, I will talk to her tomorrow.'

And then I came home, but I could not wait until the next day, so I texted her, 'How are you now, Priya di?'

She replied, 'Don't worry, beta. I am absolutely fine. I knew that if you came to know about my accident, you would be worried, that's why I didn't inform you bacha.' I felt good after reading her reply, as I was feeling awkward, that how should I ask her about not informing me, but she was too good and understanding. She understands how much I care for her. I replied to her, 'Take care my di. Get well soon.'

She replied goodnight with a smiley face emoji, and I slept.

On the next day, I was feeling bored, as Arti was not present and Priya di was unable to come and hence the workload on Kruti ma'am had increased. That night too I chatted with Priya di and texted her, 'How are you now? How was your day?'

She replied, 'Boring and frustrating. I stayed at home and that too only on the bed the whole day with no work. I hate it. I don't know how these days are going to end!' By this reply, I got it that she was feeling totally worthless due to her fracture, so I decided to do something, to make her feel happy! Then she asked me, 'How was your day?'

I replied, 'Same like yours – boring! Without you and Arti, classes are like jail.'

She replied, 'So sweet of you, but you must study. And by the way, where is Arti?' I replied to her,

'She went to her hometown, and di, don't mind, but I feel no sir is teaching, everyone is just doing their publicity. In classes, everyone in the faculty is like sweet talks only, just doing their business!'

She replied to me with a smiley. She told, 'I am also frustrated to sit at home.'

So to divert her mind towards me, I asked her, 'Shall I share something?'

She replied in the affirmative. But before it, I asked her, 'Do you believe in God?'

She again replied with a yes and also added, 'Especially Radha Krishna.'

So I shared the incident of Arbaz's mischief to her and even about Arti's belief in Ganesha. She enjoyed it.

I thanked her for giving me so much time, she replied with the usual smiley and blessed me. Lastly, I asked her, 'Do you have any boyfriend?'

This time she replied in the negative and asked me, 'Why are you suddenly asking such a question?'

I replied, 'If you felt bad, then I am extremely sorry.'

She replied, 'No my dear, I didn't feel bad, but why did this question come to your mind all of a sudden is what I want to know!'

So I replied, 'I am five years younger than you, and when I lied about Neha as I felt Arti was attracted to me, you studied my face almost immediately. This is only possible if you have similar confused feelings in your times, or maybe you are in love with someone, so I just asked.'

She replied, 'Oh good, I didn't mind at all and I am again impressed by your way of thinking, but if you use your brain in your studies, I am sure it will be too helpful to score better in your exams.'

I passed her smiley.

She added, 'I understand you because you are like my younger brother and you always call me di, so I feel good with you. And other than this we are of the same caste, so it's nice to chat with you, and the most important factor is that your nature is caring, and you are understanding even in this age.'

I replied, 'Thanks di, from today onwards, I am your younger brother only, even I would love it if I did any mischief during classes and my di would pull my ear. I would love to be scolded and guided by my di, better than my ma'am.'

She replied, 'Obviously my brother, but don't let sir know that we have such good personal relations because I am working there so I have to do whatever he says.'

I said, 'Ok, and how are you feeling now?'

She replied, 'Very nice, now that I have my younger brother.' We wished each other a good night and slept.

On the next day, though Arti was not present, I studied as my di told me. I had a test on that day, I almost got all answers correctly. I was too happy with myself and this was due to a gain of self-confidence given by my lovely Priya di.

At night, I texted her, 'Hi.'

She replied, 'Fine.'

I hadn't asked her how she was but she had replied fine which indicated that her mood was not good.

So I replied to her, 'My di, I will not ask you how was your day, because I got it from your one-word message, but you can ask me the same question.'

She replied, 'Smart boy! How was your day? And how did you get it from just the word 'fine'?'

'My day was superb. Though I was missing Arti, I kept your words in my mind, so today I gave almost all the answers correctly. Even sir was impressed today. And all this happened only because of you and your blessings. And I got it, as you just wrote 'fine', not 'bro', so I think you forgot whatever we talked about yesterday.'

'*Oye*, I didn't forget anything, it was just I am working less, and you know that *Khali dimag shaitan barobar* [Empty mind is devil's workshop]. So, I have a foul mood without any particular reason.'

'Oh, I thought today you will miss me the whole day just like I did. Leave it di. Maybe I expected too much.'

'*Oye*, I miss you, my bro. I thought of texting you at noon itself, but then I called Kruti ma'am, and she informed me that you have an oral quiz today, so I didn't want to disturb you in your studies, my dear brother.'

'Okay my lovely sister, but at present, I am with you, so please feel relaxed.'

'Whole day I am relaxing only. I am tired of it. Anyways I am happy that my brother studied today, even scored well in the test, and followed my instructions.'

'Di, can I ask you a favour?'

'Sure. But tell me what you want?'

'First promise me that you will fulfil my wish.'

'Ok *baba*. Promise.'

'From tomorrow you have to start writing something... a poem, blog, story or diary, whatever you wish, but you have to start writing. I know you have a very good talent for writing. Until your leg does not get well, you have to use your hand and heart in the best way you can.'

'Malav'

'Yes di.'

'How did you get to know about my interest in writing?'

'*Aapke Radha-Krishna ne aake mujhe bataya.*'[Your Lord Krishna informed me.]

'I had forgotten the fact that in my childhood, I always used to write a diary about each and every moment, but I don't know when I stopped it. How did you get that?'

'Di, we have a good mutual understanding as we have almost similar thinking. Your nature is also caring and emotional. I love to write a diary, so I guessed you will love it too.'

'No, Malav you are smarter than me. Yes, we both have a similar nature, and even I like to write, but at your age, I was not able to think like you. You are smart dear. By the way, what are you writing in the diary?'

'Everything. Whatever happens in each and every moment and whatever my heart says, I write it. I even wrote whatever we talked about yesterday, and whatever we are currently talking about. So, in the future when I read it, a smile will appear on my face. I believe that each day our maturity increases. Like when I read the first page of my diary, I always used to laugh and miss my best friend Praku. Similarly, when tomorrow I will read all this, I am going to laugh about my immaturity. What did you write about in your diary in childhood?'

'I used to write poems in childhood. But it was all in the past. As you made me remember my talent, now you have to tell me what I should write about if I want to start again? I mean which topic I should write on. Give me some suggestions.'

'Anything like love, dreams, friendship, relationship, about me, generation gap, situations, etc, just hold your pen, and write whatever your heart says.'

'Ok, my dear brother. I will fulfil my promise from tomorrow. Thanks a lot for such a piece of good advice, now I have a little work at least on the bed.'

'Good di, but stop thanking me else I would stop talking to you. Now you sleep, I have to study.'

'Ok. Text me whenever you sleep as I want to know up to when my brother was studying.'

I agreed and replied with a good night smiley. That night I was very happy and excited as I made my di happy. And in that excited mood, I don't know how I got too much energy to continue studies till early morning.

At 5:00 again Priya di texted me, 'Are you still reading?' I replied in the affirmative again.

'Oh, my dear boy, please take care of your health too. Now you better sleep.'

'Di, I have to attend school at 7, so if I will sleep now, then I will not be able to wake up. So, I will sleep sooner tonight.'

'Okay dear, but please take care, and if classes are not important today, then you can skip them and sleep till noon. And I know how the other teachers are teaching. So, if you feel it right, bunk today.'

'Let's see di. By the way, why are you up so early?'

'Just my eyes opened, so thought of asking you.'

'Ok, now you go back to sleep, and I will continue my schedule.'

After attending school I directly went for my tuition, but I was feeling odd, not due to weakness, but due to the classes themselves. As I had joined classes for the entrance exams of IIT, but now I was feeling that these classes were not well equipped to prepare students for such a great exam, and another reason was that in reality no such atmosphere existed here. The fervour and zeal for IIT existed only in Kota, Rajasthan. I realised that grade eleven was almost over, and I had not even gained 5% confidence to crack the IIT. Another reason behind this was my dependency on classes as from childhood I studied myself only but I had joined classes for the first time when only 4 months remained for my grade X board examination. But I continued with them in grade XI. But instead of studies, I was surrounded by a new atmosphere of CBSE type schools, girls, frank atmosphere, which I had never seen before. Whatever I am scoring here, I can score better by reading at home on my own. These all thoughts were going on my mind, Kruti ma'am interrupted me, 'Malav, are you ok?'

'Yes Ma'am, what happened to me?'

'You know Malav, Priya ma'am is a good friend of mine. She called me especially to take care of you due to your lack of sleep issue last night. And see your eyes, they clearly show how tired you are! So, you should go home now. You have a test to take but I will keep the question paper for you till tomorrow.'

'Ma'am don't worry I am fine, and I am prepared for the test. Please let me take it today itself.'

'Then before you take it, go have an orange juice, else I am not going to give you the question paper.'

'Kruti ma'am, I am fine.'

'Malav, you are still a child. Don't be over smart and prove that you know better than me. Let's go together to have juice, I know you will not go alone, so I am joining you.'

'But ma'am, you might have something more pressing.'

'For me, you are more important.' Initially, I was shocked, but later I was smiling and feeling good. Who wouldn't feel good when his ma'am would take care of him? Finally, we had juice at the juice centre; in between she rejected 15 to 20 calls, just to make me drink the juice. In the end, she called Priya di and said, 'Your brother is the same as you. He cares for everyone except for himself. Until today I never saw his strong efforts towards studies but now that he has started then he is not ready to apply brakes. But don't worry I am taking care.'

After break time, we started walking back towards class where I said, 'Kruti ma'am, I am sorry that your work suffered because of me. Though you had work, you came with me just because Priya di was worried.'

'My child, do you think that I joined you just because your Priya di told me? No, my child, I came with you because I felt right to come with you.'

She put her right hand on my left cheek and continued, 'Even I would love to accompany someone who is so pure-hearted and caring. ***A lovable person is always loved by everyone, dear***. And don't worry about my work, though I am working here, without me and Priya these classes can never go ahead. Nobody was ready to do the management job here.' I attended the test and stood second in my class, though it was a different thing that paper was too easy.

Then at night, I texted Priya di and she replied on the spot, 'Today no chatting. You have to sleep Malav.'

'Yes di, I know, and I am on the bed only. I just wanted to know whether you started writing or not?'

'Yes beta, I started but it will take 5 to 6 days to write something accurately.'

'Ok di, Guddy night.'

For some days, the same routine followed, that was, I went tuition and chatted with Priya di at night, and every day my reading increased and hence my confidence, but along with it my feeling of wasting time at such classes also became strong. I knew that I could do better on my own though I know that the time has already passed, but at least I could prepare for AIEEE on my own. But at the same time, I didn't want to leave tuition because I will miss my di and Kruti ma'am a lot. For them I am more important than their work, and then it's obvious that for me, the time spent with them is more important than studies. After all, I know myself, I can study only when I am happy, and I will be happy only when I will be in touch with them always. Anyway I need some more time to think about it, but yes currently I am missing my Arti a lot. Come back soon dear.

Ten days passed thus. Priya di and I chatted almost every night. One night, she texted me one poem which was written by her.

After reading her poem on *'Khwab woh parinde'*, I actually understood the meaning of dreams. I gave her nice compliments for her poem. Slowly, we both became attached to each other. As I don't have any sister or brother, she was more than a real sister for me. One night, she told me that she wanted to share something with me.

I replied, 'Di, even I want a break from studies, so tonight we can chat for a long time.' She agreed to this. After dinner, we both started chatting. Her first message, 'Malav, some days ago, you had asked me whether I have a boyfriend or not? At that time, I was afraid, but now that you are my little understanding brother, so I want to share it with you. Yes, I have a boyfriend. We both love each other too much and we want to marry each other.'

I felt too good to know this and I replied to her,'Oh my di, it's so nice that you have someone special in your life who loves you a lot and wants to marry you. Thanks, a lot, to God for blessing you with true love. Now, I would like to know about your love story in detail didi. I would love to hear your love story. Please if you feel it right can you share the details of your love story?'

'Beta, you are not going to believe in my love story!'

'Why not Di? I will as I trust you more than myself.'

'Dear, we fell in love without even looking at each other. Do you believe that it's possible in our current generation?'

'Of course, Di, though I don't know much about love, from childhood I knew love is not in beauty, it's a feeling. Actually I have seen a lot of romantic movies, but everyone says that movies are different from real life, but I believe stories came in one's mind after experiencing reality itself. Yes, movies do not only include reality, but they contain more than reality, but that is for the entertainment of the public only. But I believe the concept in their mind comes from reality itself.'

'Yes, dear you are right.'

'So, can you share your love story with me now please? I want to know more about love. How did he meet you? How did he propose to you? When did you realise that you are in love with him? What is his name?'

'*Bhai*, calm down. I had never seen such eagerness in anyone to hear my love story.'

'I just know one thing about love and would love to know more about it. I still remember that one dialogue from the movie *Hum Ko Deewana Kar Gaye*, "*Pyar ehsaas hai. Woh ehsaas hi hai jo do insaano me marte dam tak apne life partner ke liye rehta hai.*" [Love is a feeling. A feeling which exists between a person life-time in his heart for his other half.]'

'Yup, my bro. I even have the same feeling for him. I met him on yahoo chat. We both used to chat a lot. But slowly I realised that I was too attached to him. So, I started avoiding him. I stopped coming online. But on my birthday, I again came online (just for him), but you know the whole day he was online but he didn't wish me, and even we didn't chat anything. Lastly, when I was going offline, I texted him a good night, and his reply came. Guess what?'

'Birthday wish?'

'No, he directly proposed to me. I was on cloud nine. He was feeling the same way. But I didn't reply to him because I was frightened.'

I want to reply, but you know that in our Sindhi caste, a daughter's love marriage is hard to accept for parents. So, I shared everything that had transpired with a friend of mine who called him and told him that I had feelings for him, but was afraid about my family. So, he got my cell number from her, and called me after a few days and again proposed to me. Tears came in my eyes. Though I was crying in a very low voice, but he heard it. And told, 'Dear, stop crying! I am not forcing you for anything.' But I was not able to stop my tears.

So, he said, 'If you can't stop crying, then I would be unable to stop myself from coming to your home.'

I asked, 'What? Where are you?'

'I am standing below your building.' I ran towards the balcony to see him.

But he interrupted me, 'Stop. Don't come to the balcony.' I stopped.

He asked me, 'Do you love me?'

This time I became strong and replied him with a yes. As soon as I said yes, he didn't speak a word for two minutes and then suddenly the doorbell rang. I panicked. I was having mixed feelings, as I ran towards the door. On the one hand, I was happy that I was going to see him finally and on the other hand, I was panicking as I was alone at home and was concerned about what the neighbours would think if they saw me alone with a boy. Finally, I reached the door and opened it. There was a little boy with a bouquet and a card in his hand. I said, 'Hello.'

He replied, 'Don't worry Priya, I know you are alone at home and I will not meet you till we both don't take the final decision about our marriage. I will not take any such step due to which either you feel uncomfortable or ashamed. Whatever your colour, whatever is your look, I know your heart, and I know I love you. I am Sindhi, older than you, with a good job, so I know your parents will agree once we prepare ourselves. I love you Priya.'

'I love you too.'

He replied, 'Ok, I am going back.'

'If you wish I can come to meet you. You came for me from Bombay, at least I can come from my home.'

He replied, 'No need for it dear. I just came to console you, to gain your trust which I did.'

'But I had wished to see you once.'

He replied, 'If it's your wish then how can I refuse it? You can come to the balcony. I am in black t-shirt. But I can't see towards you dear.I entered the balcony. He was too dashing. And I respect him a lot because he kept his promise. He didn't turn his face even once towards me. Finally, he went and came after two months to meet me officially after informing his parents that he was going to see a girl for himself. We decided to meet in a temple because we wanted to start our new life after taking God's blessings. The first time he saw me when he opened his eyes after praying God Krishna. It was our first date.'

I replied to her, 'Oh my sweetest sis, I assure you that he is the perfect guy for you because he loves your heart.'

'Yes. I know bro, he is my Krishna and I am his Radha.'

'So, when are you planning to get hitched?'

'At that time, I was pursuing B.Com, so I didn't inform my parents. But within this year I am going to tell everything to my father. I know he is also Sindhi, but maybe due to love marriage a little bit of a problem could arise.'

'Don't worry. Everything will be fine. True love always triumphs. In this generation also, such true love exists, I salute him, dear. I want to meet him. What is his name?'

'His name is Krishna and you know that in our caste after our wedding our first name changes as well so I hope my future name would be Mrs Radha K. Keswani.'

'Oh didi, I will pray for your every wish to come true.'

'You know you asked me once why I had woken up early morning. I woke up to wake him up. He had to catch a local train at 6. So, every morning I used to wake him up.'

'*Aaye haye mai mar jawan aapke pyar par![Aww]* Now he is your life. I want to meet my jiju.'

'I promise you that whenever he comes to meet me next time, I will introduce you to him.'

'Di, the amount of trust you showed on me, had never been shown by anyone before me. You shared with me your life's great secret. Thanks a ton, di. Though I am a child, I may not understand every situation that you are in, but I promise you that I will try my best to understand you in every relation and situation. And I would love to do any help if needed at any time.'

'Oh my dear bro, though you are small, your nature, innocence, caring attitude, and pure heart make me feel that you are able to understand and that's the reason I shared everything with you. I Love you bro.☺'

'Love you too.'

That night I was very happy. I felt good to know about her secret, and about true love. I even felt better to know that she felt I deserve to know about her secret. My happiness forced me to take one promise by myself and that was that I will go to the Ambaji Temple by foot in the early morning once she gets engaged with him. Now, my eagerness to see him has increased manifold as I want to tease her. My happiness increased when Arti's text came that she was back in town. I was too excited so I don't know whether today I could sleep or not, but yes I know that my dreams tonight will be very sweet.

The very next day exactly after 12 days, I met Arti. I was happy to see her. At the end of class, Kruti ma'am, Arti, and I went to have some snacks.

Then finally the night came when Priya di texted me,'I am coming to re-join classes from tomorrow.' I became happier. Finally, my eagerness came to end, and I saw my di. She came dressed in a white dress, looking similar to an angel. She was beautiful, gorgeous, lovely, and attractive. I bowed down and touched her feet; she blessed me and gave me love by placing her left hand on my right cheek. We didn't talk as sir had entered the class, so forcefully I need to go inside the class. Finally, one night while chatting with Priya di, I expressed my frustration and I accidentally informed her that I was not satisfied with the classes.

She replied, 'If you don't like to study in class, then you better leave it.'

'I don't like classes, but I was not wishing to quit because I am afraid that I will be far from all of you. So, I am confused.'

'You are an idiot, Malav. Studies come first dear. Relations and friendship are not related to studies. No matter wherever we will be in the future, we have a strong bond between us, such that we will always be in touch with each other. You are too emotional dear. I know you are attached to me, but if you behave like this then how will you behave when I get married.'

'Di, *behna ki bidaai me kaunsa bhai nahi rota?* [Who won't cry in sister's marriage?] But at that time I would be as happy as you would be with the one whom you love a lot.'

'Malav. Enough. Don't make me emotional. Think practically in this issue.'

The very next day, after our classes ended, Kruti ma'am, Priya di and I went to have snacks, where they wanted to talk with me.

Priya di said, 'Kruti, please ask him what he is doing and what he wants to do! If I am trying to make him understand, instead of understanding he makes me emotional. It would be better if you explain it to him.'

So, Kruti ma'am scolded me in such a way like she was my guru, she told me, 'When we were not in your life, then did you think like this ever? You are not even 20, and then you are thinking of each and every relation. I know its well, but at the present age, to think about studies are much more important, these are the years which decide your career Malav. If you don't like classes, and if you feel you can do better at home, do it. Think practically. We all are friends; we will always be in touch.' Her words affected me a lot.

I replied to her, 'Yes ma'am, I have a feeling that I would do better on my own.Not for IIT, at least I can try for any NIT and for boards. Again, now I want to become self-dependent. Thanks for scolding me like this and making me understand what I really want to do. I am not going to attend these classes starting tomorrow itself.'

Finally, I decided but my mood was not so good, as this was my last day with them.

So Priya di pointed towards me, but told Kruti ma'am, 'Within a minute I am going to make him feel good.'

I was guessing but was not able to predict correctly. Finally, she told, 'Kruti you know, Malav loves to serve every elder, especially me. Today I had not called my elder brother to come to receive me and you know, the doctor had strictly warned me not to drive a vehicle, so I had not brought my vehicle.'

I smiled, and said, 'It means, I am going to drop you today. Yuppie!'

She both smiled. I took blessings from both, and then I along with Priya di went to Radha Krishna temple which comes on the way only, then I dropped her. I even informed Arti about my decision. Initially she felt upset, but then she even supported me. Thanks, a lot, to God for giving me three wonderful angels in my life. *Kruti ma'am*, *Priya di*, and last but not the least *Arti*.

CHAPTER FOUR

Manish's Entry in My Life

I left classes, but Pradeep continued. I started to read by myself. As it was the time of the board examinations for our seniors was going on, so Kruti ma'am and Priya di were busy. I used to chat with Arti almost the whole day. In the beginning, she used to say that she is missing me. Later on, she told me something new, that she got a new friend at classes who resemble me, his nature was the same as mine, shy and simple. His name was Manish. Though Arti was just my friend, I felt possessive for her. Every time we chatted, she had just a word in her message, i.e. 'Manish'.

Even now she said, 'He makes her miss me.' I told myself, 'Now she needs someone to miss me!' But I didn't allow that matter to affect me till I noticed that even Priya di and Kruti ma'am praised him. Finally, I decided to meet him, and even Arti was indirectly forcing me to do the same. After a few days, it was Priya di's birthday, so I decided to meet him on the same day. The day before her birthday, for the first time Krishna Jiju called me. I was so happy to talk to the person who truly loves my sister a lot. He never met me, but then also he gave me one responsibility to deliver a bouquet to Priya di as a surprise gift from his side. I was too excited that he considered me the one for that responsibility as he knew how much I respected both him and Priya di. I missed my online test for his work. That work was more important to me. I was overjoyed after completing his work. And now we were just waiting for the birthday of our princess so we can check whether the bouquet will be delivered on time or not.

It was delivered late by an hour but Jiju still felt happy and so did I. And the most important thing is that Priya di was unaware of all this. In the evening, I went to the classes to meet her. She was again in the new white dress. Again, she was looking like an angel. I gave her a gift. When she opened the wrapper and found a diary, she passed me a lovely cute smile. I really loved it. Afterwards, we had a small party. In the end, Arti came along with Manish. I finally met him and exchanged numbers with him as Arti forced me for the same; even I put forward my efforts for his friendship. After meeting him, I realised that I was the same as him when I was in grade ten and also before that when I was with Prakash, a very reserved person with a limited number of friends. One shocking news which forced me to believe that there is some strong relationship between him and me as his and my name starts with 'M', we both are shy, have the same dressing style and hairstyle, basically everything is common. Everything was fine, but what the hell? We both got to know that we were born on the same day too! God why didn't you make us twins? It was shocking to me because I was experiencing such a coincidence for the first time in my life. Lastly, I took Priya di's blessings and came back home. It was day well spent. May God give Priya di a long and a happy life.

My excitement from the previous day was still was not over, as I was overjoyed with Priya di's birthday celebration. I started to chat with Arti, I expected we would talk about yesterday's celebration, but she just asked me about Manish and whether I had liked him. I replied to her in the affirmative. Anyways, it sometimes happens, if she had thought only about me, she would have easily got that I want to talk about yesterday's celebration, not about Manish. Some months passed. I continued to be in touch with all of my three girlfriends. Sometimes I used to go to meet Priya di, in the Radha Krishna temple which was exactly at the midpoint of our homes.

My birthday was around the corner. I was too excited because I want to surprise both of my teachers. Yes, neither Kruti ma'am nor Priya di knew about my birthday. Priya di was out of town due to some family function and she was going to come back on the same day. At last, it was the day of my birthday. I woke up with my Mom's kiss on my forehead and lots of wishes on my phone from all of my friends and especially Arti. I became ready and took blessings of my parents, and then walked towards the temple for the blessings of Lord Krishna. I followed towards class where Manish and I bowed down in front of Kruti ma'am and took her blessings.

She asked, 'What is the occasion?'

We both shouted, 'Our birthday!'

She smiled and added, 'Oh! What a good coincidence!'

Arti, Princess, and we birthday boys already had plans for our celebration, and we even invited Kruti ma'am for the party but she denied as Priya di's train was running late and she couldn't leave her classes, and hence finally Kruti ma'am informed her and she wished us on a call itself. We started celebrating our day. Starting with a lunch in McDonald's followed by a walk in the garden, on the beach, playing games, eating sweet corn, taking rides, wandering, driving, shopping in malls and ending the day with sweets such as ice cream. I enjoyed it a lot and even I have one new friend now, Manish. I spent a full day with him, and hence I was very impressed by him. At night, I read Priya di's message.

She apologised as she was unable to meet me on my birthday. I replied to her saying that it wasn't a problem and we can celebrate it whenever we meet next. She replied with a smiley. Now from two, we became three good friends. Almost everything, every matter was shared between the three of us, Arti, Manish, and me. I still remember on 10 July, it was the first night of my life that I didn't sleep and continued to chat for the whole night and that too on the group. At 6:00, Manish and I slept, but Arti was so excited that she didn't sleep and directly went to thank Ganesha. It was a crazy night. Though initially, I was feeling bad, when Manish entered her life, I felt a constant change in her behaviour which hurt me sometimes. Even when I needed her, she was not noticing me because of the excitement of talking about Manish, but I don't know. At present, I just know that she is happy with mine and Manish's friendship. Yes, this is also the truth that I did friendship with Manish only under pressure from her, but now maintaining a friendship with him is my duty. **Life teaches us that friendship changes, but it makes us comfortable only when we accept that change given by it (life).** Now we all three are equal for each other. Once, Arti shared about a boy, who harassed her in her childhood. He was from Bihar. In frustration, she even used to eat chalk sometimes which once resulted in her contracting a severe jaundice. She had not informed anything about that boy and the reason for jaundice to her family. So, Manish and I made her promise her that she will not do any such stupid thing from now onwards and we decided to take care of her in that matter. But she declared that she will handle him herself, so we didn't force her, as neither of us were her 'boyfriend'.

One day we decided to meet as a lot of time had passed since we all went out somewhere together. Also, both our teachers were ready to join us. Firstly we three, Arti, Manish and I met and then we noticed that Priya di and Kruti ma'am were waiting for us, so Manish told us, 'You both go upstairs, I have to collect a bag from the ground floor, and then will join you.'

Arti said, 'No, you go and come with the bag then we will go together.'

Manish said, 'I told you I am coming.' Arti, 'I said that we will go together.'

I interrupted both of them and said, 'Manish, go and collect your bag fast, and Arti let's walk slowly so Manish will join us before we reach.'

Now whatever I am going to write is a too small thing but unfortunately, I noticed it *yaar*. When we both were walking slowly towards upstairs, I was saying something and soon Manish joined us, but he saw and hence he waited for my talk to complete, but before I ended, suddenly Arti interrupted me and asked Manish about some different topic. So, I felt bad that she was not listening, and Manish had no other option other than replying to her and hence they both started talking and I had no other option but to keep silent. Anyways, Finally, I met Priya di after a long gap, and hence took blessings, and gave her chocolate which I always used to buy for her before meeting her. Then all of us entered the garden. In mischief, I proposed to Kruti ma'am, and then we played games, had several photo sessions, etc. and enjoyed a lot, but along with it many times I felt ignored by Arti due to Manish's presence. In the end, we came back to the classes as Priya di had to collect her bag from there, so she went upstairs till that time, only me, Kruti ma'am, and Arti were there as Manish already went home since he lived too far and it was night already. We all were in a mischievous mood, so Kruti ma'am hugged me from the back and asked Arti, 'How are we both looking when we are together?'

She replied with weird expressions, 'Not so bad, but not even good.'

Kruti ma'am replied, 'Why? Why? Are you feeling jealous because I hugged your lover?'

I interrupted ma'am and said, 'What ma'am? You are teasing her with me; if you really want to tease her then you have to choose someone else!'

She replied with confused expressions, 'Whom are you are talking about?'

I replied looking towards Arti, 'I am talking about the same person because of whom Arti is unable to see her friends in front of him and it is none other than our Manish.' As soon as I completed my sentence, she held her handbag, and with a good amount of force, she hit her bag in my stomach and even blushed.

But at the same time, Priya di came back and asked Arti, 'Hey, Why are you beating my little brother?'

She complained, 'He is teasing me with Manish.'

Priya di said, 'Now, it's too late, so everyone must leave for home.' Priya di was coming with me along halfway, and we paused for some time at the panipuri centre as per the wish of my Priya di. And then we went for ice-cream, where we got a seat for sitting, so we sat and she asked me, 'What happened dear?'

I replied in negative casually.

She replied, 'Beta, I noticed you upstairs and even in the garden. I am your elder sister, you can share it with me.'

I replied, 'Di, I don't love Arti, and still sometimes I feel possessive about her. Sometimes I feel that I am losing her due to Manish though I know we both are friends, they both are friends, so this feeling should not exist in my mind or heart, but I don't know why?'

Priya di, 'My dear bro, such feelings are obvious, even I noticed that unintentionally but today many times she ignored you, and who told that possessiveness for friends does not exist. Don't worry, she will not go far from you, at this age sometimes attraction occurs. So, she is a little bit attracted to Manish, but she knows how important you are for her, you both have been friends more than a year now.'

'Hmmm... But di, I am scared if I fall for her, then?'

'Don't worry beta, you are still a child, you all are not mature enough, so you feel sometimes that it's love, else if you had fallen for her, then you had not waited till now. So before love, be mature.'

'Hmm... Not only mature, understanding and responsible too.'

'That you are, that is why you completed the task given by your jiju, and did not even give me a single hint that you did that to surprise me.'

By listening to this I felt shocked and she put her lovely hand on my cheek. I felt nice and I said, 'Thanks a lot di, for understanding me in each and every matter.' Then the first time I ate ice-cream with her hands and then we both went home. On the very next day, at noon, when I just laid on my bed for a small noon nap, suddenly my cell phone rang, and it was Arti. I felt weird as it was the first time she was calling at this time.

I picked up the call and said, 'What happened dear?'

'Nothing, I know it's an odd time, but I felt like calling so I did.' 'Oh, say!' 'No specific reason, you are sleeping, right? Sorry.'

'*Arre*, it's fine, I just came on the bed and I was thinking something.'

'About what?'

'About my morning dream today.'

'*Arre wah*, tell me na please.'

'No, it was about you and your dad, and you will feel bad after listening to it, so sorry.'

'I will even feel bad now as you are hiding something from your best friend.'

'But it even includes something about Manish, and I don't want your bag in my stomach. I have only one!'

'Oh so sorry for that, I know yesterday in mischievousness I hit it with little force, but I promise nothing like that will happen. So tell me about your dream, please. And everyone has one stomach only.'

'Though I know that Manish and you are not of the same caste, your family is different, but in my dream, I saw that you were sleeping and suddenly your dad entered your room and woke you up and asked you whether you want to marry Manish or not?' Then my eyes opened and the dream ended.

'Oh, couldn't you have waited till I answered my Dad?'

'I still can't believe that how can your dad ask you so? It's not possible as I know your dad.'

'Actually from many days I wanted to tell you something but you are unable to understand me whenever I put efforts to start to tell you the same.'

'If you can't initiate, how can I know that you want to tell me something? Tell me, dear.'

'I know sometimes I ignore you due to Manish, but I am so sorry, I don't know that. I didn't know when I fell in love.'

'What? What? Tell me again.'

'Malav, I love Manish.'

'Once more please.'

'I love Manish.'

'Dear Arti, you don't know how much I am happy for you, he is the perfect guy. As a friend, sometimes I am worried about your future life. You are childish so will your husband be able to understand you in that way? But if it would be Manish, I am too happy, I know him at least he is not a cheat. So you told him or not?'

'No, I want him to realise it himself.'

'Oh my dear, I am too happy for you.'

'Malav, I hope your morning dream comes true.'

'Sure my friend. Now I am not going to sleep. Arti now, I understood why you were feeling happy when I told you about Neha. I want to dance with you yaar.'

'*Paagal hai*, I love Manish.'

'Hip hip hurrah! Now I will tease you a lot.'

'And I am going to love it.' So after that whenever she talked, she always used to talk about him, but now I was not feeling bad because indirectly we were talking about love, the amazing feeling. A week was over, and one day Priya di called me to meet her, so we met at Radha Krishna Temple. There she informed me that Jiju is coming to meet her next month, so I became extremely happy, and in excitement, I told Priya di about Arti's feelings for Manish. Though Arti had not given me the permission, I couldn't hide anything from Priya di. Priya di was happy to see me happy but she said,'Beta, this is not the right age, though I believe true love can happen in any age.'

'*Arre* di, relax, I know Arti. She really loves him.'

'Hmm... Anyway, now at least you are free from that nonsense thinking that you have started loving her, and later your parents will get hurt, etc, etc. Emotional fool my brother.'

'By yours and Arti's true love, I came to realize that **true love can happen anytime anywhere, but if once it happens then no-one can stop it**, so if we want to be on the safe side, then we must take precautions at the very initial stages itself. For example, I don't like the word girlfriend, so I will call her my special friend, and another precaution is my parents will not like if my girl was out of my caste, so I promise, I will love only Sindhi girl who will be younger than me.'

As soon as I told these words, a tennis ball came and hit my head near my left eye with full force such that I fell down. Priya di tried to hold me but I had already lost my mind and body control and fallen on the floor of the temple. After two minutes, when I stood up with Priya di's help, one cute voice came from our backside. 'Can I get the ball please?' We both turned together, but Priya di turned angrily. I saw one little cute boy who was wearing a costume of Lord Krishna and a peacock feather on his head and flute in his belt. Priya di started to scold him but as soon as she realized his costume, she even decremented his voice. I asked him, 'Are you playing with a ball in this costume?' He replied very cutely, 'No, actually my friends are playing outside the temple, and my best friend Sudama hit this shot. I am sorry from his side. He told me if I will come to take the ball then everyone will give me because I am a good-looking boy. So, can you give me the ball please?'

We both smiled.

I replied to him, 'Only if you tell me the reason for wearing this costume.'

'Actually tonight, I have a competition in my society in which I am playing the role of Lord Krishna.'

'Oh ho, so nice of you, take this ball, and this prasad too, and all the very best for competition.'

He replied very cutely, 'Thank youuuu!!'

He went, and Priya di asked me, '*Jor se lagi?* [Did it hurt too hard?]'

'No di, I am fine, and now almost it's dark, so we have to go, and I am surely going to meet Jiju this time.' But when I came out of the temple, there was not any place for cricket, neither stump nor ground, it was a road. I was surprised, then where are all the kids, I felt weird when I realised that it was almost dark and the ball just hit me 5 to 10 minutes ago. Anyway I would love to write this incident in my diary because that kid was too cute.

One day Manish came to my home suddenly and asked me for a walk, so I agreed. As soon as I came out of my house, he directly came to the point and asked me about the Arti's feelings for him and gave me his own promise. I can't lie in front of promises; that was my weakness. So, I told him the truth.

He replied, 'I knew this from the very start of our friendship. But this is not possible, I don't love her yaar.'

I asked him, 'But why?'

'Because I don't have any feelings for her and will never have, but indirectly she has proposed to me many times.'

'So tell her the truth, why are you increasing her feelings towards you, if you already knew this then why didn't you tell anything?'

'So what I should do, according to you I should tell her the truth so again she would eat chalk or will burn her own hands!'

'Oh, you are right Manish, she is childish and mad.'

'Malav, now I am confused, what should I do?'

'Manish I think we have to make her understand slowly.' He agreed. From that time, I stopped teasing her and even indirectly asked her if Manish doesn't love you then what she will do. And she was replying the same as we expected that 'I will die.' So in her reply, I started to scold her and tried to make her understand. But even she is not stupid, she caught us within a week and everything between three of us messed up. So finally, we decided to meet and solve everything peacefully. We met and discussed a lot but in the end, Arti stood up angrily and said, 'I love you Manish and will love you forever and I never told you or want the same from you.'

Manish replied to her, 'What if I will say no?' Arti turned towards me and said, 'Don't worry, I am not going to commit suicide, Now I am not a child, whatever I did in the past, it was my immatureness. Ganesha has given me a lot of strength now, so you don't have to worry for me.' In the end, it was decided that we all will be the same friends as before. Finally, we went home, after that day, whenever I used to chat with Arti, either she was complaining or just showing love about Manish.

She can't forget him, but let's hope that time heals everything.

On the other end, Manish was going far from both of us, he always says that we are friends, but in actuality, he was avoiding us now. This used to hurt Arti a lot and so she used to cry and I consoled and always gave her my sympathy. Sometimes I get really frustrated, but I made friends, so it's my duty to keep and maintain it, and Arti is my best friend. Some days passed the same way, finally, one happy day came in my life, on which Jiju came to meet my Priya di from Mumbai. I was so happy; I met him in the evening and saw him for the first time. I bowed down to touch his feet, but he stopped me and shook hands with me. He was a superb, dashing, and smart guy.

I brought a glass of water for him and held his spectacles so that he could wash his face. By watching this, Priya di told Kruti ma'am, 'See, how my dear bro started doing the *seva [service]* of his jiju,'

I replied, 'This is my duty as per Hinduism.' Jiju smiled. After doing some regular talks, we three went towards the station as Jiju had returned after an hour, so after dropping him at the station, we went to eat ice-cream where I told her everything about Arti, Manish, and myself. She got angry and scolded me, '*Tu kabhi nahi sudhrenge na!*'[You will never improve!] I already told you, be out of all this, at the present age, just concentrate on studies, but you all are idiots. Love, feelings, everything comes with the proper age, you all are too small.'

'Di, I am sorry, I am just sharing it and you know I am like this only, and you even liked me in this way only, I can't study if I am not happy, and I can't be happy if my friend is crying. Don't worry di, I trust myself, I will do my studies also. I will surely get admission in one of the nice engineering colleges. I am sorry.'

'Oh my dear brother, I am sorry, I know you, but sometimes I care for you as a sister, but I understand you as a friend, I trust you, whatever you are doing, your intention is always good. Just be careful, don't disappoint your parents and, don't let it affect your career.'

'My career would not get affected at all, don't worry about it.'

'Ok, my dear bro.'

'I am sorry that we diverted from today's occasion. Jiju is superb Di.'

'Today was a fantastic day. Love you brother.'

'Love you too ma'am.' This time she ate ice cream by my hand. Finally, I took blessings from her and went back home. Now onwards I started to think about studies a bit more as board exams were coming close. I decided to quit thinking about IIT and started preparing for AIEEE and MP board. And everything including studies and friends, I will manage with one schedule. Finally, grade XII was over, and my exams were good. I handled everything in such a way that I was satisfied with myself. Arti completed her grade XII exams as well but sometimes she is sad after her heart break, but I always stood with her as a friend. Finally, it was vacation time so I went for a trip to Surat where I met my Best Friend Prakash. I was happy to see him and I enjoyed a lot. I am now waiting for the results.

CHAPTER FIVE

The Beginning of College Life

Finally, all entrance exams and board results have been declared, and I got admission in one of the nice colleges in Indore, where my cousin is already pursuing final year B.Tech. Pradeep's results are not as good as he expected them to be so he decided to take a year drop as he wants to study only in NIT for his engineering. Similarly, Arti's results are also not so good, so even she decided to take a year gap and Princess got admission in a college Jaipur. Manish was already engaged in pursuing a diploma so he has one more year to complete his diploma. Arti and I are best friends again and Manish is almost out of our life.

Before going to Indore, I met Priya di and Kruti ma'am. Priya di was happy for me. She said, 'At least you have cousin there to take care of you, as in the current generation, smoking and drinking are common for every boy!'

I replied, 'Do you think that I will be addicted to such things?'

'If you even try then too it's not possible! I know you very well. I trust you more than myself.'

'Oh, so nice of you didi, but as now I am entering college, so I have a license for doing a love marriage?'

'Yes, why not? I know you are going to college for this purpose itself.'

'No didi, actually I believe that whenever we run behind anyone, life always takes it away from us, and from whom we run far, life brings it near to us. Hence I don't want a girlfriend. If I try to run behind it, life takes me away from her.'

'Very smart. But life goes as per God's plan not as per your thinking my bro!' I smiled. I took her blessings and came back home, but on the way, I met one woman, who was Sindhi and she was the mother of one girl whom I like in my school life. And since it was in my nature to help others, I dropped her home. And she lives in our area itself so when I dropped her, she invited me inside, I tried to refuse many times, but when she told me to at least say 'hi' to Sakshi(the girl whom I liked) I was unable to stop myself.

I met her almost after 2 years. She was the same as in school, simple, shy, innocent, studious, and a topper. She was reading and I asked her about her admission as I knew she had also opted for science stream. She replied, 'I am doing BCA.'

'Oh so nice.' Then she asked about me, and lastly, we exchanged our number, just casually, and finally, I came back to home. It was nice to meet her, but it was the time in school life when I liked her and that also because she was the topper, as at that time I have a mentality that good girls are those who are toppers, but today I didn't feel anything like that maybe because she was too simple. In today's generation, people must be a little smart, it's necessary.

Finally, I reached my new city Indore. Initially, I was feeling too lonely, I was in a new city, the only positive is I had my cousin there ,else not possible by me to live in a new city without family and friends. I used to meet my cousin (Dipti di), every day after college and we had dinner together every day. And at other times, whenever I feel alone, I used to talk to Arti or Priya di as I still have no friends in college. And sometimes I get frustrated due to boring lectures. Of course, when lectures are conducted in a hall where more than 200 students are sitting, how can the class be interactive!

Anyways, once in a lecture, when I felt bored, I started to think of some birthday gift for Priya di's as soon her birthday was around the corner. I was sitting on the right-hand side, last row, first chair, so no faculty was able to see me. I have in mind that the best gift is time. So, I thought that I have to give her some 'time' as a gift. Finally, suddenly while moving my eyes here and there for thinking; one thought came to my mind that I can give a Radha Krishna chart to her made by my own hand. Finally, I decided, and I became excited and in excitement, slowly I told myself, '*Bolo Krishna Kanaiya ki jai*!' At the same moment, my eyes felt on the earrings of the girl sitting on the left side in the second last row, second chair. Generally, I don't like to look at girls, but I don't know what was attracting me towards her earrings. Her earrings were so beautiful in peacock blue colour, circular, and full of designs. I didn't see her face, only her earrings, but when I realised, I took away my eyes, as staring at a girl is not a good habit. Anyway, later I came to know that as per the academic calendar, I have exams in my college, so I was unable to go on her birthday, but I continued my work of sketching her birthday gift.

From the next day, I prepared one schedule for each and every task. Once, I was preparing a chart, and then suddenly a text came from Sakshi. It was just a forwarded text, but I replied with a comment on it. So, this way we started to chat and had some casual talks about college, studies, etc. After that, she asked me, 'And say?'

So I replied, 'I am free, and if we are finished from our formal talks then I have many personal questions if you feel right!'

'Obviously, you can ask!'

'Who was your first crush?'

She replied after two minutes, 'Do you want to hear the truth?'

By reading her message, I felt some strange excitement plus panic (Oh my god, what will she say). Along with such feelings, I am not very sure but I have a gut feeling that she will say my name only. But I replied, 'Yes.'

'You.'

'Seriously? Then why haven't you talked to me?'

'Because you are shy, only talking about my science textbook, and even I was feeling shy at that time.'

'Oh, good, anyways, it's nice to hear that I was someone's crush.'

After our first chat, our friendship started and slowly we started to chat every day and all the time. Sometimes, I used to flirt with her but in my mind I was always clear that I wanted no serious affairs. Though she was also a Sindhi, but I wanted only casual flirting. I don't want any attachment. But the whole time, I was chatting only with her, so I even told her about everything, my Priya di, Kruti ma'am, Arti, and lastly about Manish. Even she told me about her best friend Aashish whom I used to play with in childhood, as everyone was living in the same Sindhi Colony. At the same time, I got my first new friend in college who was also Sindhi, her name was Bhumika.

So, in college, sometimes, when I felt bored, I used to bunk with Bhumika and enjoy snacks with her. Sometimes, one more friend Dimple used to join us. Now, I have two friends belonging to my caste: Bhumika, who was fat according to the standards of a Sindhi girl, but very carefree. Sakshi, who was sweet, innocent, and my best friend. I especially like her way of respecting others. She adds 'ji' in her message, and that thing seriously attracted me towards her. I don't know, but again I was frightened that maybe I will like her more, so I decided to chat with her less, but on the same night, she texted me, 'Today is the last day of messaging and from tomorrow no message!' So whatever I wanted was happening, but on the very next moment I felt bad, and replied to her,

'So, no contact from now onwards?'

'Why? Lord has not given us mouth and phone calls? From now, we will talk rather than chat!'

I felt strange, reading these words, I thought, '*Yeh ladki to samne se muje itna bhav de rahi hai!*'[First time, any girl is showing so much interest in me] But then for some days, I didn't have the guts to text or call her, though I was missing her too much. On the other hand, Arti always complains to me that now I am too busy in college life, but in actual I was busy in trying to make myself comfortable in a new atmosphere. And suppose if I was frustrated and Arti called and if talked about Manish, I get even more frustrated, and finally the call ends with our fight, which neither of us wants!

Anyways, I was doing my job towards the gift for my Priya di for an hour every day. College life was going well and slowly I was adjusted in a new batch and made new friends. And within a week, Dimple, Bhumika, and I used to go for an outing at least twice a week.

Once I had a bad day, as one of the professors in my college scolded me and that too not because of my mistake, but on the place of the one whom I don't like at all. I was too frustrated, as I felt helpless as it was deemed university and nobody could say anything to Sir. My frustration makes me out of control, and so I called neither Dipti di nor Priya di, I directly called Sakshi and directly said, '*Yaar*, please do whatever you want to do, but please activate the message scheme on your cell phone.'

'You said means over and out, it will be activated within the next five minutes dearji, I promise.' I was surprised and feeling light, as I said once, and she listened and even obeyed me. I was happy the first time we were talking, and she helped me to take out all my frustration, and then we talked about silly matters and continued for two hours, till my balance got over. Lastly, I thanked her and she smiled, and our chatting started again. Hence our closeness increased, and so did our attachment. So, to control myself, I told her that I like Arti a lot. And on sharing this, she told me that she likes Aashish a lot, but as his mother didn't like her, they were no more friends.

I asked her, 'Only as a friend or more?'

So in reply, she told me the actual story that, 'Actually Aashish proposed to me, but I refused. One day he went to the bridge, and texted me that either I have to reply else he will jump, so I accepted his proposal and went to save him and slowly even I started liking him. So, I like him, but I do not love him.'

'Oh, finally, I got it. You mean you are in luv with him. I mean, it's more than friendship, but less than love, right?'

'Yes, absolutely.'

Once we were playing truth and dare in chat, and as a dare, I asked her for writing those three magical words, and I was surprised when she wrote it for me just for a dare. Actually, I was enjoying her friendship, her obedient nature, her respect. Similarly, on the same evening, I asked her for the kiss in naughtiness but she refused and informed me that Aashish had once kissed on her cheeks. Listening to this I felt bad, but then I thought, why I am feeling bad, I am not her boyfriend. It's her life. She used to chat less in the night as she slept with her mother, which sometimes disrupted my mood as I have a habit to chat with her, but she went in her room at 10 and I did not sleep before 1 or 2, so till that time, I felt very bored. Though I have a huge amount of college work pending but without talking to her, I was not ready to do it unless and until there was some pressure to do it. And the other thing which I didn't like was that she had stored my name in her phone book with a girl's name, as she lived in a pure Sindhi area, so obviously in her home, talking to boys was strictly prohibited. Yes, her family was narrow-minded, even sometimes I feel she was also narrow-minded in some silly ways.

Anyways, once it was night and she was ready to talk to me as her mother was going to some function and was going to come late. Hence we decided to talk peacefully on that night. I finished my dinner soon after that night, and even she finished her work faster than usual. Finally, we both came on our own terrace and talked a lot that night. While talking, I saw a moon in the sky, so we started to talk about the moon and moonlight. Obviously, like every girl, she said, 'I like to walk in the moonlight.'

I said, 'So, let's do one thing, let us disconnect our call for five minutes, and let's imagine that we are together either at your terrace or mine and we are walking together in the moonlight. And after five minutes, we will again talk, and if our feelings are strong, we will surely have the same talks.'

'Which feelings?'

'*Arre*, feelings of our friendship dear. Feelings of moonlight. Would you like to walk with your friend in the moonlight?'

'Yes.' (I assumed she told yes with a shy smile on her lovely face.)

My imagination:

Me, 'Hello Sakshi, can I hold your hand?' Sakshi, 'Sure dearji.'

Me, 'I don't know but will you be able to understand my and Arti's relationship? Will you be able to fulfil all my expectations of my wife, my mother's expectations of her daughter-in-law?'

She just smiled.

Me, 'Actually, I know, you can do it.'

Then we walked together, no talking, only watching in the eyes of each other.

'The feeling of true love in moonlight.'

Finally, those five minutes were over, so I called her. I asked her about her imagination, she replied, 'No, first you tell me.'

So I started but didn't talk about wife and daughter-in-law, only about the relationship of Arti and me.

Then I asked her about her imagination, so she replied, 'In my imagination, we just talked casually.'

'Then I think you must have been shocked by hearing my imagination? Right?'

'Obviously, *tum to bahut aage badh gaye dearji*.(You went too ahead, friend).'

I told myself, 'Thank God, I didn't tell about wife and daughter-in-law.'

I replied to her, '*Yaar*, your word 'ji' made me go ahead to such an extent(*yeh tumhare 'ji' ki wajah se hi mai itna aage badh gaya!*) I have never got such respect by any girl, and I always expected such respect only from my wife.'

'But I add 'ji' in every word irrespective of whomsoever I talk to.'

'Yes, I know, you give respect to everyone, that's why I am afraid that what will happen if I will fall in your love with you.'

'Now Bye, Mom is back, so Guddy Night.'

'Hey, Guddy is my word.'

'I knew on the second day only that you write Guddy instead of Good.'

'Oh really, even I didn't realise it. Anyways, I always wished that whatever I was not able to notice about myself, it will either be noticed by my special friend or by my wife.'

'Ok, now bye.'

Finally, she disconnected the call. Her mom came back at the wrong time. And we went to sleep without texting each other.

I woke up early the next morning, though I was lying on the bed for a long time and thinking about the girl whom I don't know but yes was thinking about lying with her. Why I used to say more about Arti and my relation, I really don't know. Maybe I am afraid to fall in love with her, but why be afraid of love. **Love just happens; it can never be controlled by anyone.** It's a feeling and the heart is the key for that toy, hands for that key is not our hands, it's God's hand.

So why to be afraid, as I believe God always uses his hands for the holy and good work. And if I am not wrong, Love happens at this age only. I think I should share this with anyone. I have 3 options, but Priya di and Kruti ma'am are busy, so let's share this with my best friend Arti. I talked about my attraction towards Sakshi with Arti, but she didn't notice it as she was busy about the complaints of Manish. And even she was complaining about me as now I am in college, so it seems that I am busy for her, and she stays at home for the whole day as she has taken a drop year. Anyway, after a week, I am going home, hence I will meet Priya di, and will talk to her about it. And her gift was almost ready and after all New Year is also coming hence mini vacation in college so no-one will miss the chance for home sweet home.

Sometimes I felt bad, as I am busy, and maybe in actually, I was tired to hear complaints about Manish, it was intolerable for me. I want to be happy. I want to see her happy, but I don't know how it feels when someone we love leaves us. Maybe I was a little bit selfish as my heart also became sad when she was sad which I didn't want or maybe I was frightened to face her, as it makes me feel like a failure as a friend, as I was unable to help her to move on. I really don't know, so I don't want to think a lot about it. I know it's wrong, but I want time to think about that matter. I am sorry Arti. Then for the remaining week, we had our exams. So every day, Sakshi woke me up, and yes for controlling my feelings, and my thinking, I had just kept in my mind, and so writing in my diary too that following people are made for each other.

Arti, Manish, Priya di, Krishna jiju and last but not least Sakshi, Aashish.

Finally, in between exam days, one day it was Priya di's birthday. I wished her and she informed me that Jiju was going to come to meet her. I felt happy and sad as I will miss the chance to meet him. Anyways, I already reminded Arti, so she can wish on the same day, and even I called Manish and asked him, 'Hey, you know it's Ma'am's birthday?'

'Yes.'

'But do you know that Jiju is coming to meet her.'

'Hmm, No, I don't know.'

'Oops, anyways, maybe she doesn't want to inform about it sooner, as you know, it's a serious matter. I informed you because I want that if there is any emergency you have to take care of Jiju as I am not there. If requires you have to take him to your home too.'

'Yes, don't worry.' I felt good hearing this. He is still my friend, he is far from me due to Arti, but he is ready to share about anything else, except about Arti. On the day of her birthday, I was so excited, that my exam was best, though I did not read much. Even Sakshi was telling that she feels with my voice that I am flying in the sky. I realised on that day that how it feels, **whenever someone close to our heart is happy it makes our happiness infinite.** Finally, the exams were over, and I caught a train for home and on the train, I was chatting with Priya di. I asked Priya di, 'How was your birthday?'

She replied, 'Fantastic dear.'

'By the way, what did you tell your family? You already left the job!'

'Dear, at home, I told everyone that I am going to celebrate my birthday with Manish, Arti and Kruti ma'am, and even added that you are trying to come.'

'Oh ho Didi, at least you should have informed me. By chance if we had not talked today, and if I would have directly come to your home to surprise you, and then imagine what could have happened? Forget me, if by chance Arti and Manish tell something in front of your family then?'

'Malav, I am sorry.'

'Didi, it is not about sorry, I am just saying that for the safe side, you ought to have informed me if you were using my name. Anyway, forget it; tell me when I can come to meet you.'

'Whenever you want bro, but Malav, I am sorry because I lied to you. I already informed about Jiju to Manish, but to you, I informed him the day before he came.'

'What? But why? And I asked Manish about this, but he even told me no, it means he even lied!'

'I only told him that not to tell you, actually everything planned so soon that I didn't get a chance to inform you, and when I got a chance, at that time you had not received my call, you might be in a lecture or in the exam. So, I called Manish, and made him understand that not to inform you as I know you that you are possessive. I know that if he had informed you, you would have felt that I informed him before you.'

'Di, I don't know what to say!! You can never be wrong, but I must say that like at present you are making me understand calmly, in the same way, you had tried at that moment, I think I would be able to understand you. I agree that I am possessive, but I even hate lies. Anyway, it happens sometimes. Forget it, it's not your mistake; it was just a mistake of situation or circumstances. And I know, where love comes, nothing else matters! On that day, you were happy na?'

'But at present, I am sad as I hurt my little brother!'

'No didi, don't worry, I am fine. Now, make your mood normal fast, else this time I am not going to come to meet you.'

'Sorry bro.'

'You also knew that I hate sorry and thank you.'

'Love you brother.' Finally, we decided to meet on 1st Jan at her home and ended our chat. I was listening to songs and obviously I was sad because really, I felt bad for whatever happened. (Talking to myself) 'Malav, due to your possessive nature, your favourite di needs to lie to you. It's not right.'

'I am sorry Priya di.'

Sakshi texted me, and we initiated our chatting, and with my very first reply she understood that I am not fine, so she asked me, and I informed her about my possessive nature. She replied, 'It's fine dearji, some people are possessive in nature. It's no need to feel bad that you have such a nature. And it happens sometimes as per the situation, but you can also think like this, that your Priya di **loved you so much that even cared about your nature.**' She changed my mood, just with a sentence. I was the one who used to change everyone's mood by talking positively, but today she was the one who was teaching me what I used to teach the others.

She replied, 'Anyway dearji, are we guddy friends?'

'Obviously yes Sakshiji.'

'So, can we meet tomorrow?' By reading this message, I felt so happy, I don't know why. Just two minutes ago, I was too emotional, and within 2 minutes my heart was on cloud nine.

I replied, 'I would love to meet you dearji, but how will you manage as your family is not allowing even to talk with me?'

'Dearji, tomorrow I have a party at my college. Tomorrow is 31 December, so I will come from the party and will meet you and then go home. If anyone asks, then I will tell you met me on the way by chance! Don't you think its ok, if I will tell a small lie? *Itna to juth chalta hai na dearji? [Small lies are allowed, sometimes]* Please I want to meet you.'

'Sure dearji, we are meeting tomorrow.' At last I reached home. My family was too happy to see me, and so was I. On the next day, I completed the chart of Radha Krishna, as on New Year I was going to give it to my dear sister. Now I was just waiting for Sakshi's call, and as soon as she called, I was so excited, I took out new clothes, new perfume. I was feeling like I was going on the date. No, actually in my life, the first time I was going to meet a girl alone and that too with prior planning. We decided to meet at the mall, a public place, so we both feel comfortable. I got ready, took my bike, and made my way towards my first meeting. On the second signal, I saw a flower shop, so I drove my vehicle towards that shop, though I don't know what was going into my mind. I took a red rose from that shop for a moment. I even didn't think that if she felt that I am proposing to her and maybe she felt bad or uncomfortable. But when I reached the next signal, that thought came to my mind, so I took a U-turn and exchanged the red one with the yellow. Then I drove my bike at the speed of 80km/hr, I reached, she was already waiting for me. I had kept the flower in the pocket of my jeans and hid it with my shirt. She had worn a red top and blue jeans. She was looking too attractive and why not? She had come from the party. I looked in her eyes. Her eyes matched with my eyes just for a moment, and the very next moment, her eyes moved at the ground. I asked her, 'How are you?'

'Hello, I am fine. You?'

'Same.'

'Enjoyed the party?'

'Yup.'

'So, let's go inside the mall, and do some window shopping. I know that girls love window shopping.' She kept quiet and followed me. Her lips with red lipstick were looking so lovely. But as soon as we reached the entrance, she called me from behind and said, 'Malav, let's walk on the road, there's too much crowd here.'

I said to myself, '*Oh mahi ne [Oh My God]*, this is not what I had thought. I thought she will not feel comfortable alone, so I suggested a crowded place but here she herself wants to be in a lonely place. Anyways, I think at least we can talk or share our stuff peacefully.'

I replied to her, 'Sure.' Finally, we reached the backside of the mall, where no one was present; only vehicles were crossing that road, but there were rarely two vehicles in 5 minutes. I asked her, 'So, how was your day?'

'Good. Only once a year does a party happen in our college. So, I enjoyed it.'

'Then too you left the party soon for meeting me.' She smiled on listening to this.

I added, 'You know, tomorrow I am going to meet my Priya di.'

'Yes, I know. You've already told this to me 7 times.'

'Oops, sorry!'

'Don't be, I know you are too excited about it.'

'But you don't know that I am also very excited about our present first date... I mean the first meeting.'

She paused and looked in my eyes, and even I did the same. Soon, we realised that we are on the road. So again, we started to walk, and she asked, 'How's your girlfriend Arti?'

'Oh Arti, she is not my girlfriend, she is my best friend, and I knew that you know that, but you just want to hear that from my mouth.'

She gave me some angry but smiling expressions. I added, 'And I luv her, not 'Love' her.' This time she gave me confused expressions.

I explained to her, 'L for Lion and U for umbrella wala LUV her.'

She remembered and replied, 'Oh yes, I know your Luv and Love rule.'

I asked her, 'How's Aashish?'

She replied, 'He is fine, but neither he is my U for umbrella Luv nor O for orange one. And he had never kissed me. And please don't ask me why I informed you this, because I think I don't have an answer, but you have.'

We both smiled.

Just like in Bollywood movies, cold air blew near us. So I said, 'I had not haven't worn a jacket, else I would have given it to you.'

She stared towards me, paused and replied, 'No need.'

Then I thought in my mind that shall I say *'Jakad lu tumhe?'* ('Shall I hug you?') I was just thinking, and I don't know from where I got energy and I was just going to ask her this, but my cell phone rang.

I to myself, 'Oh shit. This is the same what happens in movies.' I took out the cell-phone from my pocket, and it was a call from Dimple. I received the call.

She said, 'Hey Malav, do you have some Bollywood romantic movie for this mini-vacation? Actually, my roommate forced me to call you as she needs a movie anyhow.'

I said to myself, 'I am going to see your roommate later.'

I replied to her, 'Sorry, but I am at home, not in Indore.'

'Oops, sorry.'

'It's fine.'

Finally, I was back with Sakshi, but the cold winds were not blowing anymore. And even we completed the one whole round of walk, but we both started for the second round. Again, I initiated, 'What are your future plans after college? Masters or Job?'

She angrily turned towards me and said sarcastically, 'I did not come here to talk about studies with you. Seriously you want to talk about them?'

'No, actually I want to talk about romance.'

I to myself, 'Oh shit, which word I said?'

But she felt shy, and her eyes again turned towards the ground. I will die looking at such a shy smile. Again cold air came, and this time, without being late I said, 'Hug?' But she didn't hear it and started sharing something about the party. Again, cold winds started blowing around us, and this time in a little louder voice I said, 'Shall I hug you?'

She noticed and replied, 'No need.'

By her reply, I felt she became angry, but her eyes were telling me that she was feeling shy. I was confused, and the very next moment, her cell-phone rang. That call was from her home, asking her about when she is going to come back. So finally, we ended our second round too, but I requested her for the third last one. She agreed.

I said to her, 'As this was our first meeting, so I had bought something for you.' As I took out the flower from my t-shirt, she stopped by holding my hand for the first time. I felt so happy. I was again a filmy moment with colourful butterflies fluttering inside my stomach. She even realised that I was lost as soon as she touched me, so she took her hand back and said, 'Keep it inside only.'

I said, 'Its yellow rose only, you are my friend dearji.'

'Yes, but how can I take this home?'

'You can always hide it in your college bag na!'

'Oh ok, but don't give me here, I feel awkward walking with you, and holding a rose in my hand. So, give me after we complete our walk.' I smiled. She passed a shy smile.

I said, 'I was going to buy a red rose but didn't have the guts to give it to a girl.' She passed me a smile again. Then for the remaining walk we were just watching each other, not at the same time though. When I was looking at her, she was looking downwards, and when she turned her face towards me, I looked towards the ground. The same cycle continued until our third round got over.

In the end, we smiled for such a thing we did. At last I took out a rose from my pocket, and was thinking how I should give it to her, by bending on knees, for which I was not ready, and it was yellow, not red. I was busy thinking, and she took the rose from my hand, and said, 'No need for it.'

I don't know, but I asked myself, 'Has she heard my inner talks? My thoughts?'

She said, 'Thank you; finally, I really enjoyed my real party.'

I asked her, 'What does that mean dearji?'

But she didn't reply and we both turned towards our home. As soon as I reached home, there was her text in my inbox which read:'Means, in the whole party, I was eagerly waiting for the clock to strike 5 and I am also very happy that someone gave me a rose, those 15 to 20 minutes of walking with you, were my life's best minutes ever. And yes, I luv you, (not LOVE ☺).'

After reading her text, I felt like I was flying, not having ground below my feet, but sooner I control myself as I was at home, I was frightened what should I do if my mom asks. But as soon as, the clock struck 12, I heard the voice of crackers, the shouting of children, I called and wished her, 'Happy New Year' and asked her to hold the call for a second, and ran towards my terrace where I could get privacy. But on the way, the poster of Radha Krishna had fallen from the chair due to wind blowing from the window, so I took it and kept back to its place at the chair, and closed the window. I finally reached the terrace and added, 'I love you.'

She asked, 'Which one?'

I replied, 'I for I L for L...and O for Orange one love.' After completing my sentence, my heart felt a little relaxed.

I added, 'I had not planned anything, but all of this happened in the spur of the moment itself.' But on the very next moment, my heart beat again became faster, and I felt, maybe she didn't love me as she had not replied anything still now. So, gathering guts, I asked her, 'What's your answer?'

Her sweet words ever, '*Agar na hota, to ab tak baat kar rahi hoti kya?*' ('If my answer was no, would I still be talking to you?')

Oh my god, I was so happy. I shouted, 'Sakshi, I am so happy.'

'Yes, I can feel it from your voice.' She added after a silence break on call, 'My mom is waiting for me, but I don't want to go.'

'I know you don't want to go, but now I am yours forever. So, don't worry, go and join your mother.' I heard her smile's voice. So, I added, '*Yeh to shy wali smile hai*...[oh, you are blushing] Go dearji, I love you.'

'Dearji, I wished instead of asking if you had hugged me. (*Kash jakad liya hota muje apni baho me*) Bye, Guddy Night.'

I was so happy! When I cut the call, I saw 7 missed calls from Arti. Oops, I called her back. She received and asked, 'Whom you were talking to?'

I replied, 'No one. Anyway, Happy New Year!'

She replied loudly, 'Happy New Year.' I continued to talk with her, for around 10 minutes, and lastly, I was back in my bedroom, after wishing my mom and dad. Though I stopped myself a lot not to be a committed person and even I lied a lot regarding Arti to her (Sakshi), and even she lied to me, but in the end, *feelings won, and we lost.*

And these feelings are not of attraction, but that's also the reason. I felt them for the first that day while talking to her in the moonlight, and secondly, today when I proposed to her in an unplanned way. Surely, this is natural love. I am too happy. I was unable to sleep the whole night, and even Sakshi was not able to sleep, as I texted her at 2 AM and in reply, she passed me a missed call. Love her :) *That walk with her changed my life.* Now I am no longer single, and I am really feeling great. Thanks a lot, Godji, for giving me such lovely love and such a pure-hearted simple girl to love!'

CHAPTER SIX

Sweet Moments

It was 1 Jan 2010, New Year. For the first time I went to Priya di's home, she felt too good to see my surprise gift for her (the Radha-Krishna Poster), which I made for her with my own hand, using decorative borders, needle and thread. Then we chatted a lot about Jiju and the experience of date cum birthdays. And lastly, she asked me, 'Any special friend in your new college?' I informed her everything about Sakshi. Initially, she was shocked, hence she asked, 'Don't you think, you have proposed to her too fast?'

'Yes didi, but it was unplanned.'

'Yes, I can understand, else you would have taken my permission. Anyway, it seems this time you are serious.'

'Obviously didi.'

'No Beta, I am just trying to say, that in the current age, we are unable to differentiate between attraction and true love.'

'Yes didi, I know, that's why I avoided myself many times, by assuming that this is just an attraction, but I don't know what happened suddenly yesterday, and I proposed to her; so this is real love didi.'

'I know my brother very well, so now be with her for your entire life but concentrate on studies too dear.'

'Don't worry didi, now I have my life partner in my life and in actual my luck will convert from good to best from now onwards.' Then I met Priya didi's father, and lastly, she asked me about Manish and Arti. I sadly informed her whole story of them, and added that now Manish is no more in contact with us.

Lastly, I showed her a picture of Sakshi and me together, which was edited by me. She commented, 'You both look nice together.' As I am now a committed boy, as soon as I reached home, I inform Sakshi and my daily routine was to talk with her on call for about 1-2 hours every night. Initially, we decided not to think about the future, family matters, marriage, as there were still chances for family problems to occur and we didn't want to think about any problem in our new relationship. But we both don't know, when we started to dream about our future home, our future dreams and she used to call me, 'Jaan', 'Jaanji', 'Hubby' and various other terms of endearment and even I used to call her Sakshiji.

Finally, I was back in Indore, but we continued to talk daily. I was woken up by her every morning and she controlled almost my entire day's schedule from morning to night. Then it was our first valentine's day but we just wished each other, as we both are shy. She also called me at 12. After the first semester, I made a new and good friend in college named Ankita, who used to study with me, so I always used her name to tease Sakshi, and then very cutely I always used to ask her,'Are you feeling jealous?'

She replied very cutely, '*Thodi Thodi!* [Little bit!]' Such a reply always makes my heart skip its beat.

In even semester, we have a cultural week, which I enjoyed a lot. I even made many new friends in college. Among all the different days, the school day was my favourite, and on that day, along with me, Ankita also participated in a school day competition. She used to live behind my PG, so we used to study and hang out together. After exams, I had to go home on next day, as my summer vacations had started, but one night before it, I was talking with Sakshi on the terrace, suddenly I saw towards the moon and asked her, 'Dearji, I am the Moon, you are the moonlight, the stars are my friends, the sky is my family, but who is the Sun of my life?'

She instantly replied, 'Of course your Priya di.'

On hearing this, I felt so happy, as she was able to hear the words of my heart. 'I love you dearji, I love you a lot. You know, I want to confess one thing.'

'What?'

'You remember in school life, while we were in grade X, I always used to take science textbooks from you, by arguing that I have an old one?'

'Yes, I remember.'

'And do you remember, once by mistake I had kept Sandesh's love SMS in it, and you returned it after 2 days when I asked for it?'

'Absolutely.'

'Dearji that was not kept by mistakenly, it was my plan.'

'Oh, so you love me from grade X?'

'Maybe, actually no, at that time I was attracted to you, I don't know when it converted to love.' Finally, my summer vacations began and in 2 months we had

2 good news. The first was that Sakshi's sister soon to be engaged and another was that on the day of her engagement, my wait was going to over. No, no, though the line for me towards Sakshi was open from that day, luckily Priya di was also going to get engaged with Krishna Jiju on the same day. And yes, Arti is still in the picture, she knew everything about Sakshi. Arti and I used to talk once a week, and every time we talked, she complained that I don't give her enough time. Anyway, one whole year of engineering got over. I don't know when it got over, but at the end of it, I made at least one nice friend in college and that too a girl.

Firstly Sakshi invited me to her sister's engagement, and even I was going to attend it, but when I informed her about Priya di's engagement on the same day, she got double happy, and before I could say anything, she shouted, 'True Love Won, Yippee.' We both were very happy on that day. I attended Priya di's ring ceremony with Kruti ma'am. Both were looking awesome. Girls look very beautiful after applying make-up, but even Jiju was looking great in front of her. After cutting the cake, Priya di called me and asked, 'Happy?'

'Of course didi, very much.'

'Yes, your face is reflecting your happiness, even more than my face.' (*Tere chehre pe mujse jyada khushi jhalak rahi hai.*) After dinner, I took blessings from both Priya di and Jiju, and left for home, as it was too late and even Kruti ma'am needed to go home. But as everybody knew I am crazy, so around 12:30 AM the road was empty, I stopped the vehicle, before I reached home, and danced too much without any music to express my happiness to myself. I was very happy with my di's engagement. True Love had won. I called Arti and informed her, and she also felt happiness. On the very next day, I met Priya di at the same temple where we used to meet. She showed me her ring, and pulled my ear and said, 'Kruti ma'am and Jiju both were saying that you seemed to be happier than me! Idiot, Why so happy?'

'Didi, you don't know this is true love, in which two people who had not even seen each other, but still fell in love, and didn't leave each other's hand till they got engaged. Didi, in the present generation, *finding true love is not less than finding a fortune*, and you both *not only found it but have stuck to it, it is a great victory of life* didi.'

'Malav, I love you brother.'

After some days, I fulfilled my promise of going for a walk to the temple in the morning which is 12 kilometres way from home. My friend was going to join me, but he was not able to wake up in the morning. I was woken up by Sakshi at 5 in the morning and I couldn't break my promise, as Godji had united my didi with her true love, so I started off alone.

In the thoughts of true Love, I don't know when I covered 12 kilometres in 2 hours. I was too happy. After going back home, Sakshi asked me to rest, but I decided to meet her as she was going to Pune the very next day for summer vacation. We met in the evening, and for the first time she fed me ice cream with her hand and so did I. Then, we both shared our experiences of our sister's engagement. Then it was time for going home so I asked her, '*Aaj to jakad lu?*'(Can I hug you at least today?) She passed me a shy smile. I tried to hug her, but I don't know why I still didn't have the guts, and this time, she passed me a smile on me.

So, I added, 'Let's leave, we don't have the guts to hug at public place. (*Jao, jao, yeh hug wug, hamare bus ki baat nhi*) Love you.'

She closed her eyes, 'Love you too.'

Finally she went for a month-long vacation, and strictly told me not to call till she came back, but she used to call when she got a chance. So, I too decided to go to my mama's home in Gujarat. But I had to do one important work before leaving - Arti.

Arti and I had not been talking properly from the past few months, so this time we needed some more time to understand each other's situation, hence we decided to meet. We met in the garden. She was upset, frustrated and I knew it. But she was trying to behave normally; anyhow, I knew that I had to help her take her frustration out. I remembered how I was feeling when in the past she always used to talk about Manish. So, I started talking about Sakshi, and continued to praise her though whatever I was telling about her was real, like she was too caring, lovely, and she always respected everyone. Finally, her the limits of her tolerance were reached and she shouted in frustration, 'Yes, nowadays, you only care about Sakshi. I agree she is your love, but family and friends also matter in life. The whole day you are busy in college, and you are spending your entire cell-phone balance on her. Have you ever thought about what I feel? How bad have I been feeling from the last few months?'

'Yes, I know what you feel. I know that each and every day, you are feeling lonely without Manish and you still hope for him to comeback in your life. You still miss him.'

By hearing such words, she cried and said, 'You did this knowingly? (*Jann bujh kar mere samne tariff ki na Sakshi ki?)*'

'Yes, I did that so we can talk about what you want to talk about, what you have in your heart. I know you since the last three years dear, so at least I know when you feel what!'

'You are too bad Malav, you were busy the whole day in college, and no-one has hurt me ever like Manish. I promise, from today, I will never fall in love again, and not only that I will not make friends too whatsoever. I don't need anyone in my life. I know you are always with me. I hate you Manish.' Completing these words, she burst out with tears, and at the same time, my cell phone rang, but I took it from my pocket fast and disconnected it though I saw it was Sakshi, and hugged Arti.

She cried a lot, and after some time she stopped a little, I gave her water and said, 'Dear, this time is so bad, time always plays with a person and their feelings. Just a second ago, we feel happiness, and after a moment we are sad. You are telling that you are not going to make friends in college just because of one person but you can't avoid the goodness of many other people. Still in this world, there are many good and honest people. I promise you that you will be unable to stop yourself from being a friend of a good person, as goodness attracts everyone. This all is in the future, but always remember, there is one person for you forever, me. And you know how much I can do for you.'

'Yes dear, I know, I wish Manish was like you.'

'Oh, now you like me?' (*Acha, aaj tuje bada mai pasand aa raha hu!*)

'Yes friend, today I understand your possessiveness when I used to talk about Manish in front of you, but you are too good as you are not giving me the chance to feel possessive for you, but I have always made you feel possessive. Today I learned one new thing from you, that possessiveness is intrinsic to human nature, and it's a friend's duty not to make our own friend possessive for us like you did.'

'Arre, I just did.'

'That was just to take out my frustration, else I know you always take care of all your friends so he or she doesn't feel possessive for you like you tried to hide Sakshi's call from me and disconnected it. Although she was calling you after 10 days, you missed a golden chance to talk with her just due to me dear.' I smiled.

She added, 'I am also your friend, though sometimes I am not that understanding towards you. I Luv you Malav, you are always with me.'

'Promise me, whenever you miss him, you will call or miss me, to forget him.'

'Obviously friend, you have supported me in every phase in my life.' Finally, I dropped her home and hugged her once again. It was easy to hug a friend as compare to special friend.

After coming back to home, I gave Sakshi a missed call and she called back within a minute and asked the reason for my not having picked up her call earlier. I replied, 'Actually I was with Arti, and.'

'Ok dearji, I know you very well, I know that you don't want to make any of your friends feel that after getting a special friend you have forgotten your earlier friends. Dearji, I am happy with your thinking, you have to keep your friends as first priority. Where will I go?

Also, after we get married, you and your whole time would belong to me only. I just called to hear your voice.'

'Love you for understanding me dearji.'

'How is Arti now? Do you need me to talk with her if she feels low?'

'No dearji, I handled her this time, I will inform you if it is required in future.'

'Don't worry dearji, she will get on it soon.' We talked for a while, and then she went informing me that after Pune, she was going to Haridwar. Then finally I came back home, and after a few days even she returned. In between, we talked a few times. One special incident worth writing about is that when she was in Haridwar, once she kept her cell phone on charging in the balcony. But within a few minutes, she saw that her cell phone was taken by one monkey. She ran behind her for almost an hour in the whole city. Finally, the monkey stopped at one tree. She was running without wearing her slippers and that too at noon, just because she knew that her cell-phone was the only one option for her to communicate with me and she couldn't stay without passing a missed call to me at least once in a day. Finally, like in storybooks, she acted like she threw a cell-phone and that monkey copied her and she ran towards her mobile and kissed it opening my photo. We decided to meet on my birthday as I was going back to my college after three days of my birthday. We met; it was my birthday plus our date. She came in a yellow dress, with green dupatta. She was looking very beautiful. I had worn red jeans with a blue shirt. I was looking very funky. Anyways, she was my *jaan* (life). She had surprised me with two beautiful gifts. One was a mug, which she bought from Haridwar, and another was a birthday gift, a very lovely statue of Radha-

Krishna because she knew how much I loved Radha-Krishna.

It was first time she sat behind me on my bike holding my chest. First, we went to the bridge, where we walked for some time, then I took her to a garden, but it was uncomfortable for both of us though there were many couples present. I think all of those couples were older than us. So, I took her to the nearest coffee shop. Then after some time a call from her home came, and we had to end our date. I tried to hug her, but as soon as I reached near her, I put forward my hand to shake and thanked her for the lovely gifts. I enjoyed my remaining birthday party with my family and my friends, including Priya di, Kruti ma'am, and Arti. Yes, truly I missed Manish as his birthday was on the same day, and even we celebrated together last year. I even noticed this on Arti's face, but she tried her best to express her happy smiles, as she was happy for my birthday, but she was feeling sad due to the absence of Manish. Anyway, soon my college reopened and along with that, I got news from Arti that she had got admission into one of the nice colleges in Chennai having cleared its entrance exam. Finally, it was time for her to begin her new life. Ankita forgot to wish me on my birthday, though I was not expecting that in one whole year, I don't have even one bestie in college who will miss me during the vacations.

On the very first day of second year, we were introduced to our new subjects. After a week, juniors entered our college, so I became a senior. Once I went to meet Ankita in classroom no.2 (as we both were in different classes) during break time, but she was not there. Beside me, I saw one girl who entered the same class, and she called her friend. She asked her friend, 'Hey I have two junior roommates, so do you have extra drafter?' But her friend replied to her in the negative. Hence, she turned back towards the classroom gate, I saw her 'oops' expression like she did any mistake innocently. It was a lovely expression. She was in a grey coloured top with colourful bubbles printed on it and black coloured leggings (not jeans). She was a little overweight and was wearing very large thick spectacles. When she went out of the class, I even noticed her cute butterfly shaped earrings. Both of those were matching with her top. At the same time, Ankita entered the class, with 2 or 3 of her friends; I asked her about the result and said hi to others. But that drafter girl again entered the classroom, and one of Ankita's friend informed us, pointing towards her, that she was the topper of the first year. She came towards us only and asked the same question of drafter to the same girl who informed us about her rank and once again she got the same reply, and I saw the same expression on her innocent face. I can't control this time, so I called her, 'Excuse me, I have one extra drafter if you need.'

'Yup, I need.'

'I can give to you tomorrow.'

'Sure, but I need tomorrow only as both have EG Labs tomorrow, so will you surely bring it without forgetting, else I can remind you tomorrow morning before college if you can give me your contact number?'

'Sure.'

I gave her my contact number, the first time any girl asked me for a number, and that too a topper. Then she asked my name.

I replied, 'I am Malav and you?' Along with these words, I put forward my hand for a handshake like a gentleman.

She even joined my hand and replied, 'Ishika.'

'Congrats for the best result,'

'Thanks.'

'Nice to meet you.'

'Same here.'

In this conversation, we had very gentle smiles on our faces. Except when I congratulated her, along with gentleness happiness was seen on her face. She was so happy with her result. In the evening, I teased Sakshi that a girl took my number from herself. But she knew that I am teasing, so she was not giving any reaction. I repeatedly teased her finally she replied, 'Not to worry dearji still you don't have her number. You gave her your number, but you have not taken from her.'

She was right. To defend myself I said, 'So what, she is going to call me tomorrow morning, so she will wake me tomorrow morning.' I tried to tease her that tomorrow anyone else was going to wake me up, which you were doing from the last few months.

But in reply she said, 'Oh, so nice, it means tomorrow I have a holiday from that work.'

'Why? Who told that? Obviously not. Whosoever comes into my life, but in the morning it's your lifetime duty to wake me up?'

She smiled. The next morning, Sakshi woke up a little bit late and called me, 'Still sleeping? Why I thought your new friend woke you up.'

'Dear, *uske intezaar me to mai soya hi nahi!*' (For waiting for her, I didn't even sleep.)

'Okay, now stop your acting, and wake up, I am not going to allow you to sleep for a moment more.'

'Only 10 min Jaan.'

'No Jaanji, I am already late, I need to go college, wake up fast!'

'Okay, my sweetheart guddy morning.'

'Guddy morning, now go and get ready within half an hour and keep the drafter in your college bag now. Catch you later after college.'

I gave her drafter in college, and she thanked me for it and even said, 'Sorry, forget to remind you.'

'It's fine. By the way, in which batch you are?'

'I2.'

'Oh, even though I am in the same batch. And you are the topper, so I am very sure your notes would be nice and completed every time.' She smiled.

I said, 'I need notes for DDC, actually I bunked its first 2 lectures, but I am enjoying that subject now.'

'Ok, I will give it, but in the evening, as notes are at the hostel.'

'Ok, so can I have your contact number?'

'Oops, I forget that you don't have it, I am giving you a missed call.' Finally, I got her number. That night, I again teased Sakshi, and now I have her number. She interrupted me, 'You know Jaanji, why do I wake up late?'

'No, why?'

'I was having a very sweet dream of ours.'

'Oh, good, then tell me na?'

'It was 6 August and your birthday. We had planned to meet, but I was unable to come, so you were not talking to me. Then in the night, you directly came to my room and celebrated your birthday.'

'How did I come in the night?'

'Obviously by the pipe.'

'I don't know about the pipe, but I will surely fulfil your dream, by celebrating my birthday once again on 6 August. I will come home as it would be a Sunday, and friendship day, plus we have a holiday on Monday due to Janmashtami (Lord Krishna's Birthday).'

'Oh, my sweetheart, love you a lot.'

'I must fulfil every dream of my jaan.'

Life is going very nice. Even I started to get involved in my college. I was happy with my college life, and with my batch mates' unity. Everybody in my batch was unique. Everyone is intelligent. One loves one subject, then another one loves another, one loves singing, one loves dancing, and another loves mimicry. Our whole batch was full of entertainment and we had a lot of fun together. Everyone is talented, and no one can be compared with the other. Let us introduce each and every one. I know this is a diary, but I am writing all this so that when I read it in the future, I would like to know how life changes, how mature we are today as compared to yesterday. In college, Raj was on the roll after me and one Punjabi girl whose name was Prity, but we used to call her *'sikhdi'*, *'bhatinda ki sikhdi'*. We three were the most talkative people in our batch. Pratik was too intelligent practically, but very silent. Vishal was also intelligent and was the singer of our college. Ishika was also in our batch, but she used to talk very less. Her nature is very shy. She just used to roam with her roommate, who is also our batch mate,

Dolly, who was so cute, slim like a doll. So sometimes we used to call her Doll or Dhingli. Dimple was not in our batch, but she was still my friend, though Bhumika left the college.

The first internal exams of the third semester got over and I came back home. After many ups and downs, anyhow I managed a meeting with my love. Arti was in Chennai, Kruti ma'am was busy in her new job, Priya di went to her hometown, so on friendship day, I have just one friend in my city, i.e. my love Sakshi. I decided to give her maximum happiness this time, after all this was her dream. We met in McDonald's and she was in a purple coloured dress, and this time even I was in blue, contrasting to her purple colour. I had already asked her what she was going to wear. Initially, I bought only one ice-cream, from which we shared. Slowly we started exchanging sweet nothings. I had already informed Ankita about the date. So, I called her to tease Sakshi. Ankita, on the other hand said, 'Idiot, enjoy your time with her rather than wasting your time teasing her. Say romantic lines to her instead of calling me.' After ending my call, Sakshi said, 'At least when you are with me, don't use your phone.'

'Oh, like if I say, you are going to switch your cell-phone off!' She stared in my eyes and with a beautiful smile, she took out her cell-phone, and switch it off and added, 'When I am with you, I want to be just with you physically and mentally both.'

'Oh dearji!' I took out a friendship belt and friendship ring and placed them in her hands.

She said, 'I thought, you will propose to me, but here you are celebrating friendship day! No problem, I am happy for that also☺'

'Close your eyes!'

'Why?'

I stared at her and smiled. She closed her eyes. I took out another grey coloured ring on which 'Love' was written and wore it on the third finger of her left hand. She opened her eyes and got super excited. (Though it was of plastic ring) I added, 'Will you marry me?'

First, she saw in my eyes, and then she smiled, bowed down her eyebrows, and shyly said, 'Yes.'

Oh my god, I can die on her way of shyness. I kissed on her left hand. Her eyes became big and she turned here and there, I interrupted her action and said, 'No one has seen us dearji, everyone is busy with their partners.'

She again smiled shyly. I said, 'On 6 August, we will celebrate our anniversary dear, as you know, 1 Jan is already the new year day. I can't merge 2 occasions in a day.' We continued our sweet talks for some time. I will call her 'Shona' after we get married. I love my future wife Shona lot. Then we decided to go for a long drive.

While I was taking out my vehicle from parking, I said, 'Hug me, when I drive.'

She refused.

I added, 'Okay, if you are uncomfortable hugging me, then it's fine.'

'When did I say that?' I laughed and asked, 'Dearji, what will you call me after marriage?

'Hubby.'

'No, I am asking in Sindhi, in front of my parents. Translate the word hubby in Sindhi.'

'No.'

'Please.'

'No, I feel shy dearji.'

'From now onwards, I will talk in Sindhi only with you, still you don't call me with that word.'

I started my bike and she sat on the back seat holding me. I started to drive slowly, but then suddenly, I gave full acceleration and speed crossed 82 km/hr. She said, 'What are you doing?'

'First call me in Sindhi.'

'No.'

I increased the speed upto 90km/hr and replied, 'Your wish.'

So she hugged me tightly, I decreased the speed. I shouted, 'I love you Sakshi.'

She even shouted, 'I love you too.' And hugged me tighter than before and she even kissed me on my back. In excitement, I again raised my accelerator, this time, she said, 'Aeydha, *Ghaadi dhire halaayo na!*' (Hubby, slow down the vehicle na!) By hearing such words from my love in our mother tongue, gives me a lot of happiness. I stopped the bike and turned towards her. She felt shy and turned her face down. My heart wants to kiss her on her lips, but I don't have such guts. I was going to hug her, but two-three vehicles passed by us, so she said, 'It's a public place, let's go back.' I started biking, and she sat hugging me tightly. While driving I took her right hand and kissed it 2 to 3 times, and even once I bit her. She even kissed me on my back many times. At last, our date was over. But we both were happy, as we were unofficially engaged now.

6th August, Our Engagement: MALAV and SAKSHI

\#

7th August, Janmashtami. I decided to spend this day with my mom. I love to hear a story about Lord Krishna, My mother used to call me *Kanaiya* in childhood though I was shy in nature, but in childhood, I was very mischievous with girls. I have to catch a train for Indore on the 8th morning. So, I enjoyed the whole day with my mother, lastly, at night, I went out in my society for the celebration of Janmashtami. We have 7 *Dahi Handi* at different places in our society. My friends called me to join, but I refused as they were all wet. I don't want to be wet; I just want to enjoy watching. They completed breaking 5 Dahi Handi, but when they tried for the 6th, they fell many times, but they all were unable to break it as it was a little high. So, in excitement, I shouted, I will try. My mom tried to stop me, but I ignored her in excitement.

I covered my right hand with a handkerchief, and in the group, I was on top, and gave a punch to the handi, and dahi fell over me, and I along with my friends became wet. I really enjoyed it. Now the last dahi handi remaining, for which I supported my friends, in which I stood on 3rd from the bottom along with my one friend, only the last person above me was going to come up, but before it, we became unbalanced and fell. As the handkerchief was still in my hand, so my right hand became a little turn on land, but I was fine. But my mom got worried. Again, we gathered, and this time I stood on the ground and helped everyone to go up. Finally, we succeeded. I enjoyed it a lot. My mom saw my hand, but I told her that it is absolutely fine. After ending our celebration, we came back home, and I went for a bath. After the bath, my mom again looked for my hand, it was a little swollen.

My mom was worried to see it, and asked, 'It seems to be a fracture, how will you go tomorrow? Paining?'

'Mom, don't worry, it wouldn't fracture, and it is just swelling. And no pain, so let's see tomorrow.' That night, I slept with my mom, as she was too worried about my right hand. But I was unable to sleep, and as time passed, my pain was increasing. At 3:00 AM, it was almost intolerable; hence I realised it was a severe accident. Initially, I thought I should wake my mom, but then I thought, if I can divert my mind, then the pain will be less, and even mom will be less worried. Obviously in the current age, after our mom, we have just one option to divert ourselves: that is our girlfriend. So, I sent a blank text message to Sakshi.

Soon she replied, 'What happened dearji? Any bad dream?'

'No, just wish to talk!'

'Why, what are you thinking?'

If I will tell the truth, she will also get worried, so I replied, 'Thinking about you na! So, I am not feeling sleepy!'

'Oh, about me. What you are thinking about me dearji?'

'That, how sweet you look while sleeping!'

'Sweet?'

'And sexy also!'

She sarcastically said, 'Don't you get it little early?'

'This time unable to see you shy, that's why! You girls, when we are romancing, you feel shy and when we don't, that time you try to make our mischief dirty. I mean sexy.'

'That's the reason, it has been said from a very old time, that it is not easy to understand girls by boys.' My right hand was paining, so I diverted the topic from romance to normal, and we continued to chat till 5:00 AM. Now, my pain was seriously intolerable, Sakshi even texted me, 'Jaan, we have been chatting from the last 2 hours, but I don't know why I feel that you are not fine. Before sleeping, you were happy for the celebration of Janmashtami, then I tried for the romantic mood, but maybe you felt shy as our new relationship, but then too I am feeling something strange. You don't want to chat, but you even don't want to let me go. What happened? Is everything fine?'

'First promise me, you will not worry!!'

'By reading your last text, obviously I will worry Jaanji, Please tell me fast.'

'Last night, during the celebration, I fell, so my right hand is paining a lot.'

'Oh My God, and you were hiding it from me, dearji, wake your mom up na, she will give you some medicine! From the last 2 hours, you are tolerating your pain alone; I am never going to talk to you if you repeat it ever. Wake your mom now up.'

'Dear, she will also get worried like you, so I didn't want to wake her.'

'Jaan, she is older and experienced. She can give you at least painkillers, so you can sleep well. Your right hand is paining, and you are chatting since the last 2 hours, this is absolutely not fair. Whenever we feel sick, it's better to be a little child, because no-one can ever love you like your mom. So, for my sake, wake up to your Mom.'

'OK dearji.'

Finally, I woke my mom up and she gave me medicine and even hugged me, so I slept peacefully. When I woke up, it was 9 AM, I saw my cell-phone and read Sakshi's message, 'Jaanji, today I am taking my phone to college, so please after completing your sleep, go see a doctor, and give me updates, I am always waiting for you. Take care. Love you.' My mom helped me to brush, she was right, we have to go to the doctor at night only, but I only refused. Finally, I got ready and walked to the doctor along with my parents, where we are waiting for the x-ray reports.

At that time, Sakshi's call came, 'Where are you?'

'Don't worry; I am in the clinic only and waiting for x-ray reports.'

'Too much pain?'

'No dearji. You are with me and so are my parents; this pain has no guts to be in my hand. Pain frightens from my loved ones.'

'Jaan, text me as soon as the report comes out. I am going back to the lecture. Love you.'

At last, reports came and my mom was right, I had a fracture. I have a thick and hard plaster of Paris on my right hand for 21 days. And the doctor even recommended my parents, not send me out of town. Finally, I had to cancel my plan of going back to college.

I texted Sakshi, 'Reports are out. My right hand needs 3 weeks rest, as it is fractured.'

Her reply, 'Jaanji, I had half a heart attack the moment you informed me about your pain. I couldn't concentrate in my studies at all. Take care, I will call you as soon as I am free from college. Please take care.' She was worrying too much, even my mom's expression was of worry and she was feeling bad for me. Weeks passed and eventually I already called Raju and said, 'Hey, I am unable to come to college due to my accident, so inform me as soon as results are out.' Due to the accident, Arti came to my home and scolded me a lot, even Priya di called and shouted at me,'You are already weak, who told you to go for breaking handi.Idiot.'

Everyone was scolding me, but I was feeling good, as I was being loved by many. Even unexpected casual friend Ishika texted me, 'Hey, I heard about your accident, how are you now?'

I replied, 'I am fine now, but feeling bad as I am unable to attend college. Break in my studies.'

She replied,'But health comes first.' I replied, 'Hmmm... And yes in studies will you help me in covering up whatever I will miss? Especially DDC?'

'Of course, friend. Get well soon.' I was happy that everyone cared for me a lot, though in college, in my batch mate, only Ishika texted, but I was expecting others too especially Ankita.

Anyways, I was happy to have friends like Arti, Priya didi and my love Sakshi. Ten days passed, Sakshi was eager to see how I am, but as I was unable to drive and even mom was not permitting me to go outside alone, we weren't able to meet. Once dad went to the office and I forced mom to buy me my favourite evening snacks from outside, so she went and I called Sakshi, to come home. But I didn't call her inside my home, as I was alone and she felt uncomfortable too, but she was shocked to see my plaster of Paris and even got little tears in her eyes. I said, 'Dearji, it's fine. I am absolutely fine.'

We talked for ten minutes outside my home only.

Then she said bye and even added, 'Thanks for arranging the situation so I saw you, finally *meri jaan me jaan aayi!*' On the very next day, Raju called me and informed me that in the first internal I stood first in my branch. Listening to this, I was so happy as I had got the first rank for the first time in my life. I informed my parents, Sakshi and friends, everyone was happy. And in maths, I had scored full marks. But in the end, I was feeling bad, because I was not in college. It was the first time I had topped but was not in college. So, whenever someone would ask for the topper, I would not be present. I missed the chance of feeling like the topper in front of the whole class. Yes, but due to my result, everyone in my batch called me and congratulated me. There was even a call from a friend, whom I was expecting, that is Ankita. At least I knew that now my value in college was doubled.

Anyway, now almost 15 days have passed, so I convinced my parents to permit me to go back to college. I was feeling bored at home the whole day, and another thing was, I already missed my college days from the last 15 days, I can't tolerate 1 more week at home. I knew now how to deal with every work, though I have POP in my hand, besides my roommates are too much helpful people. Initially, Sakshi also got angry at me, when I informed her that I am going in such a condition, but later I convinced her too. I reached college; my father came to drop me. I saw several new faces in my class, due to late admission of Diploma students. And everybody was shocked to see my POP.

Ankita said, 'I can't see you like this, so please go home back.' I replied, 'Chill, within 2 days, you will be in the habit of seeing me like this.' It was Saturday, which meant a half-day in college, so I already took an appointment for studies from Ishika. I informed Sakshi, as she wished to talk with me at noon, but studies first. Hence, I along with Ishika, started to walk towards college for study. She congratulated me.

I replied, 'By mistake I got this rank, else you deserve a trophy for always being the topper.'

'No, but I am not a studious person like you.'

'How can you tell me who the studious person is? When did you see me reading?'

'Yes, I am watching it currently, you are not well, and then too you came for study. If I was at your place, instead of 21 days, I have taken full month for rest.'

'Oh, this, actually I was feeling bored the whole day at home. And you know that vacant mind means devils mind. *Khali dimag shaitan barobar.[Empty mind is devil].*'

'And one more thing, I am a lazy person, especially in case of studies, so at least I can learn from lectures, as I know I will not study from myself.'

'So I am your lecturer today. *Acha bottle me utara hai tumne mujhe!*' [You are smart; you have used me well without even letting me know about it!]

'May be yes or might be it was Godji's wish that in such condition also, I am with you. Else, I believe whatever happens, happens for the good.' She was going to say something, but suddenly her leg turned a little and within a moment, she fell and sat on the road. All happened so instantly, that even I didn't understand and was unable to do anything. She woke up, I asked, 'Are you ok?' She nodded. But after this, we both became silent till we reached college. We both were feeling awkward.

I jokingly said to comfort her, 'Actually whatever you were going to say, it might be wrong, that's why Godji made you fall! By the way, what were you saying?'

She smiled and said, 'I don't remember, might be I was saying that you came for study.'

'Oh seriously, then it's good that Godji made you fall, once more Godji.' She laughed.

She was too innocent and adorable. I said, 'Maybe Godji want to make us good friends.' She smiled again. Finally, we sat on the stairs of the garden. We studied for an hour or two and even talked. After that time, she became a good friend. Also, one friend 'Napster' from the Diploma was also nice. Every batch mate of mine was nice and close to me as I was the topper. Among everyone, Ishika was very simple and understanding. She was even too caring as a casual friend. Though she was the topper, she never felt jealous of me and even never had the attitude of being a topper. Whatever be the reason might be my good rank or might be my frank nature but I was happy that they all are my friends. We all became now one nice group. I started getting more and more involved in college. Every night, my love makes me remember my regular medicines. Watching me happy, she was also happy. My week was over, so I went home and to the doctor. He removed my POP, and slowly I became normal as before. Then, we went back to college where we did our work in the lab together as a group. Since all belongs to a different city, so now we were not only a group but like a family. Everyone was living in that city without their family, so in the current city, we were the only family for each other. Once in the lab, I was chatting with Sikhdi. During our chit chat, I informed her about Sakshi and my relationship with her. She felt good. But after reaching home, I called Sakshi and told her about that. She said, 'It's fine. If you feel right to share with her, then I don't have any problem.'

'I was expecting this answer only from your side. But you know what I am feeling currently?'

'What?'

'Actually I feel Ishika is a better friend of me. I don't compare friends, but suppose if Ishika comes to know about this, she may feel that Sikhdi is more important for me so I think I have to inform her too, so she does not get possessive.'

'She is not your girlfriend dearji.'

'I know, but I am too possessive for my friends too, so I don't want to make my any friend possessive.'

'Okay dearji, do whatever you feel is right.' So, I called Ishika and informed her about my love for her. But I didn't inform her about the name of my special friend. I had not informed that to Sikhdi too.

She shocked and asked, 'Why did you suddenly tell me about your love?'

I answered, 'Actually I shared all this with Sikhdi, so…'

'So, you think you have to share with me too.'

'Dear, you are better than everyone else. It's not like comparing, but I can trust you, so I shared with you. I thought you will happy for me.'

'Of course I am happy for you, even I am double happy that among your friends I am on your top priority.'

'Thank you very much Ishika.' Finally I was happy. I have everyone in my life, my loving and caring parents, my best friend Arti, my caring Priya didi,Kruti ma'am, my college best Friends, Ankita, Ishika, Raju, Nepster, Dolly, etc. I was just missing my old best friend Prakash.

CHAPTER SEVEN

Roman

As time was passing, I was feeling luckier and luckier. Sakshi, who was my luck, was with me, so my power of understanding got better, learning power became more efficient and my results were a lot better too. Even our love and respect for each other was increasing. Once I was on a call with Sakshi and Ishika's call came at the same moment, so I disconnected Sakshi's call.

Ishika said, 'You received my call; don't tell me that for receiving my call, you disconnected your girlfriend's call.'

'Girlfriend?'

'I mean a special friend.'

'Chill Ishika, she understands me very well. She knew that for me, friends come first.'

'Oh, good. What a nice girl!'

'By the way, why did you call? Any important work?'

'No, I was going outside for laundry and some extra work and I was alone, so if you are free, will you accompany me?'

'Sure, just give me 5 minutes; I will be outside your hostel till then.'

'Ok, see you then,' I called back Sakshi and informed her about my talk with Ishika. She replied, 'Ok, dearji, go and tell her from my side that we both never wanted to hear that after my entry in your life, you forgot your friends.' I laughed. She added, 'Dearji, I too want to confess one thing like you did.'

'Yes say.'

'I was buying a new textbook of Science Subject only for you so that you can borrow it from me. I liked talking to you in school time also.'

'Oh dearji, Love you a lot. Muah'

'Go, Ishika is waiting for you.'

'Now, you are talking about such special moments then why will I want to go?'

'Even I wished to talk with you but my tuition students are coming for a reading, so I have to teach them. Besides, you have to go out.'

'Ok, but at least one kiss.'

'No Malav, Go.'

'Please.'

'On the phone?'

'So what? Imagine that I am with you only, standing nearby.'

'Muah.'

'You know sweetheart, my lucky number is 2.'

'Smart boy. Muah!'

'Love you a lot.'

'Now, go dearji, your friend is waiting.'

'Okay. Bye.'

I reached outside; she already was waiting for me and passed me a smile. Before I say anything, she said, 'It's fine, I can understand.' Then we enjoyed her works. Ishika had half an hour before her hostel closing time, so we decided to go for a walk. She felt hungry, so she asked me whether I wanted coffee or corn. I choose corn and added, 'From childhood, I have seen in Bollywood movies, that for coffee or tea, the hero only goes with his heroine, so I would love to have my life's 1st coffee with Sakshi.'

'Oh, Good. So, you've never had coffee?'

'Neither coffee nor a sip of tea.' She smiled, and I passed her cheese corn, 'Here comes your corn, you like cheese a lot, right?'

Her eyes became large, a big beautiful smile appeared on her face, and with lovely expressions, she nodded her head in affirmation. Then we had our corn and went back to her hostel. I said, 'You have very nice expressions.'

'Thanks, everyone says that. And even this is the reason; I can't hide anything from anyone.'

'So, it's a nice thing, friend.'

'Hmm...'

'Anyway, I had a nice time with you.'

'Same here, Malav.'

Finally, with a little break (named Ishika), I am back with my Sakshi. We shared every moment. When the Diwali vacation started, I came back home. It was the next day of Diwali, i.e. New Year's Day. So, while talking to Sakshi, I asked her about a lip kiss for the first time. She replied, 'Shut up, *Besharam[*Shameless*]*!'

'Dearji, it's a new year. No gift for your Jaan?'

'But dearji, on the phone. I am feeling weird.'

'Like you will not feel when you kiss me physically.' There was utter silence from the other side.

'Jaan, I have a cushion, you take your teddy bear, then slowly, you kiss him on his lips, I will feel it.'

Finally, I had my life's first lip kiss. Though it was not physical, but then too felt it was very sweet. The vacation over got and then it was time for the external exams. I was very happy, as we both stood first. No, not Sakshi, Ishika, I along with Ishika tied in the third semester external examinations. All due to Sakshi, she came into my life, and my good luck began.

#

On 13 October, around 2:00 AM, I was sleeping, but suddenly my cell-phone rang. I saw Sakshi's photo on my cell phone's screen. I picked up the call in worry. She was too frightened on another side. She had the worst nightmare. I told her to relax, but she was breathing too fast. I hugged her virtually. Slowly her breath came into control. I made her to drink water and asked, 'How are you?'

'Feeling better in my Jaan's arms.'

'Love you baby.'

'Please never leave me alone.'

'I promise, never.' Then we continued to talk for five minutes, and then she went back to her room. So, we started to chat as she was unable to sleep. Finally, I got an idea to relax her. I asked, 'Have you seen fire in your nightmare?'

'Can't we switch to any other topic dearji? I want to forget it.'

'Do you trust me Jaan?'

'What are you asking Malav?'

'I am asking my real question now, 'Will you marry me, my Sakshiji?''

'Of course, Jaan.'

'Then, we shall wait no more, dear. We are getting married now itself around the fire you saw in a nightmare. Let the nightmare know how much deep love you have inside your pure heart.'

'My Jaan, I was waiting for this moment.'

'Ok, so I am holding your hand and we are going to take our first round around the holy fire.''Yes Jaan, with every round, we will take one promise for each other.'

'Okay, dearji.'

Sakshi, 'With the first round, I promise that I will love you forever Malavji.'

Malav, 'I will love you too.'

Sakshi, 'With second round, I promise that my whole body and soul belong to you forever from the current moment.'

Malav, 'Same for you dearji.'

Sakshi, 'With the third round, I promise you that I will consider my happiness in your happiness, my hubby.'

Malav, 'Ok Jaanji, now from the fourth round, you should go ahead of me. And now I will take the remaining promises.'

Sakshi, 'Ji *Aeydha*.[Yes, husband]'

Malav,'With the fourth round, I promise you that till the time you want, we will be best friends only and even after our marriage, I will not touch you till you feel comfortable.'

Sakshi, 'I love you.'

Malav, 'With the fifth round, I promise you that I will never let you cry due to me.'

Sakshi, 'I know.'

Malav, 'With the sixth round, I promise you that I will never force you to do something which you don't like, and I will never tell you to come for me against your family. I promise you that your family will be mine, your every relation would be mine.'

Sakshi, 'Jaanji, I can't live without you.'

Malav, 'Now, with the last round, I want to take this round holding you in my hands dearji. So, Can I?'

Sakshi, 'Sure my hubby.'

Malav, 'Sakshiji, with the seventh round, in front of this holy fire, I promise you that I will do whatever you wish. I will live and if you want my life I will also die for you. My soul, my body, my time, everything belongs to you from this moment.'

Sakshi, 'Can you please take me in your arms tightly? Please.'

Malav, 'Sure.. Tight Hug..!!!'

Sakshi, 'My *Mangala Sutra* [a necklace that groom ties around the bride's neck]?'

Malav, 'Sure Jaan, close your eyes, I have one friendship belt, that I am going to wear you as a mangal sutra.'

Sakshi, 'My eyes are closed, and I am feeling your arms around my neck jaanji.'

Malav, 'Now, last thing.'

Sakshi, 'Please no!'

Malav, 'What no?'

Sakshi, 'I know you very well, you will be ready to take your blood out for filling my *Maang*. But I don't want to see my hubby's blood. I know you always have a red pen in your compass box. Fill my head with its ink hubby.'

Malav, 'I love you. I am filling it.'

Sakshi, 'And I am feeling it.'

Malav, 'Now I am officially your husband, and it's night. So, May I?'

Sakshi, 'Yes, officially you are my husband. So yes, you may.'

Malav, 'I would love to take you in my bedroom holding you in my hands on this precious night.'

Sakshi, 'Sure my Jaan.'

Malav, 'From today, it's my duty to take care of your health. You are too tired today. I just want you to sleep tightly in my arms. No romance tonight dear. I know, it's not the right time. We are still small. Romance on our honeymoon Jaan.'

Sakshi, 'Okay Hubby ji. As you say. I love to lie in your arms.'

Malav, 'So Sakshi, here I took you in my arms, I am sharing my blanket with you. I want you to sleep in my arms; no romance, only tight hugs, and a nice sleep.'

We went to sleep around 5:30 AM. From the very next day, we are talking and behaving like husband and wife. We respect each other. She started to take my advice/permission in some matters and we used to talk about the Karwa Chauth. Besides every night, I asked her for a good night kiss.

#

One evening we were talking, and she informed me that she was having pain in her stomach. She has been having it for the last few days. So, I asked her to go for a doctor, but she refused, and added, 'I know why it is paining, so no need to go for a doctor.'

I asked her, 'Why? When did you complete your MBBS?'

'Dearji, I know.'

'Okay then tell me, what is happening?'

She has no answer.

So, I guessed and asked her, 'Ladies problem?'

She replied in affirmation and asked me, 'Have you studied chapter 14 in grade IX biology?'

I replied, 'That one which was omitted in our school? Obviously not! It was for self-study, and I never read self-study portions.'

'Why? No even in your tuition classes?'

'Jaan, don't you know that I didn't go to tuition until grade X?'

'Yes, I forgot. It means you don't know anything.'

'What I don't know?'

'About ladies problems?'

'It's a ladies' problem, why should I know? I am not a lady. What are you talking dearji?'

'Nothing leave this topic.'

'Ok but take care.'

After some time, I was thinking repeatedly about what actually Sakshi wants to tell me. According to her, who was I? Was I that bad guy who knows about ladies' problems? How can she even think of her hubby like this? I felt bad, but then suddenly something clicked into my mind, she asked me about the knowledge which was in a book.I didn't stop myself and called her and asked, 'Jaan, what was in that chapter? Do you think that chapter was necessary for me also to read?'

Sakshi, 'Jaan, that chapter was necessary for everyone to read.That's the reason it is given in syllabus.'

'Okay, no problem, if I had not read, you can teach me, whatever is written in that chapter.'

'No, I can't!'

'Why? You are my wife.'

'But Jaanji, I can't.'

'It's my order, my wife.'

'That's not fair. Okay but only on one promise?'

'What?'

'You will not ask anything in between and even after I complete. And I will teach you tomorrow evening. Okay?'

'Okay, I promise I will not ask any doubt.' I eagerly waited for the next day. That whole day, thousands of questions were arising in my mind. I was feeling like I am in a swimming pool of questions. Am I too innocent or am I going to be a bad person or was I already one?

I was worried about myself. But finally, evening came, and with a lot of force, finally, Sakshi started to teach me using the technical terms of that subject. Slowly she informed me what an ovule is, what an egg means, and what bleeding indicates in the case of girls. The first time ever, I understood that advertisement about sanitary pads for the girls. I was shocked to know about all this. I didn't have even 0.1% of knowledge about sex. Lack of such knowledge is a bad thing. I understand why Sakshi felt uncomfortable, though she is my wife. I understood the mood swings of girls. At the same time, I was feeling too bad for girls. I watched boys making fun of girls in this matter, but this was the first time I was getting it.

From that moment, respect towards girls increased manifold in my heart. I salute them; they tolerate a lot. Sakshi, 'Jaan, relax.'

'No, I am feeling bad for girls.'

'Jaan, you know, you should be a girl.'

'What? Why? No, I don't think I can tolerate like you all girls. You all are great.'

'I am saying this, because of how emotional you are! Jaan, this is the truth and girls are like this only. Don't think much about this Jaan.'

'I have no words for you Girls.'

'Jaan relax. My hubby, I need a hug. Tight hug? Can you please?'

'Sakshi.'

'Stop crying Jaanji, else I am not going to talk. My hubby is so sensitive.'

'Hug me please.'

'Love you with a tight hug!' Finally, we ended our chat. After a long time, I just need time. My time with my diary, with my thoughts, and my feelings.

Hi diary. Today I learned a new thing. Life taught me a lot of different lessons. First, the trust shown by Priya di on me was never shown by anyone else. Secondly, the time with Arti made me realise about my possessive and caring nature. Thirdly, Kruti ma'am made me realise how sensible I am. If I am sensible, I am an understanding, pure-hearted person, and then I am thankful to you Godji for making me like this. Also, I am glad that you sent Sakshi in my life, but please forgive me as I am not satisfied with your discrimination between boys and girls. You made two different types of people: Male and Female, I do not totally disagree with you, though I know that after bad times only, we realise the meaning of the good times; the sunrises only after it sets. Closeness results after we get to know about the distance. So, I know you are not wrong, forgive me if I am notable to understand you because I believe you. You Godji, in every way, have always shown me the correct path, and it is my responsibility to understand your way. Today I came to know something which I needed to know much before, so my sympathy towards girls has increased. It's your rule for girls. Even you can't change it. Nobody in the world can change this cycle. So, I am Sorry Godji. I promise you, from today I respect them more. Thank you, Sakshi. I salute each and every Girl.

From the very next day, I became too careful to talk with every girl, that in mischief also, girls shouldn't get hurt due to me. But then again Sakshi made me understand, 'Jaan, you are over caring. You got to know about this yesterday, but every girl including me has accepted this truth. So, dearji, accept this truth and be normal. Else your change will only make girls more uncomfortable. Jaan, try to forget this or leave this to the ladies only. It's just important that you know, so in case you show gentleness. My hubby is already a gentleman. I love you always. You are mature now.'

'Yes, Sakshi, you are right. Thank you. Lastly, I don't know, but I am sorry.'

'OK, Apology accepted, now, never talk about this matter with anyone. Okay my hubby?'

'Ok Jaan. Guddy night.'

'I know you are always right, guddy instead of Good. So, you don't know, even I started the same for you.'

'Oh my Jaan, I never realised about myself too. I don't know when I started to write Guddy instead of Good.'

'Jaan, mummy calling. Talk to you later. Love you. 😲'

#

Sakshi was my wife in my imagination. We both were acting like husband and wife from the 13th of October. Once, her mom was out of her town, so we decided to chat the whole night. On that night, I offered her to go to Switzerland for our honeymoon in our imagination. She agreed. It was 8th December after midnight. That day was our life's first roman(romance). We had pre planned our first night.

Sakshi,'I don't believe it. You are taking me to Switzerland. I love you Janu!!'

Malav, 'Darling, I know I am shy but now with you I realise, some feelings are unstoppable.'

Sakshi, 'Jaan, no more words. I thought I need to teach you everything, but you know that girls are girls. In this case, girls are shy, not boys.'

Malav, 'Jaan, Can I hold you in my hands? I want to take you to our bedroom in my hands.'

Sakshi, 'My arms want to wrap around your neck.'
Malav, 'Jaan, close your eyes too.'

Sakshi, 'Ok my hubby. Muah😘'

I took her inside our decorated room. Sakshi, 'Oh Jaan, roses! Love you for creating a romantic room.'

Malav, 'Janu, tonight I need to do roman with you.'
Sakshi, '☺'

Malav, 'Aww, I should die on your shy smile.'

Sakshi, 'Don't see me like this Jaan. I feel shy.'
Malav, 'If you wish, I should switch off the lights.'

Sakshi, '*Neki aur puch!*'[Why seek the permission of one you are doing a good turn to?]

I ched the lights off.

Sakshi, 'Why are there two blankets in this room?'

Malav, 'Who cares, today we are one, so we will wear only one Jaan.'

Sakshi, 'Want milk?'

Malav, 'Ofcourse, but you have to feed me with your hand.'

Sakshi, 'Here's your Milk Aeydha'

Malav, 'Aeydha☺. One sip for me and one for you.'
Sakshi, 'No, one sip for me and two for you.'

Malav, 'Jaan, as you say.'

Finally, we finished our glass of milk.

Malav, 'I want to kiss you on your shoulder, neck, face. Can I please?'

Sakshi, 'Yes Janu. You can kiss me anywhere. I am totally yours tonight. Tonight, I want to merge my soul with yours.'

Malav, 'Ok Jaan. I am kissing you hard on every part of your face. I am holding your hands tight.'

Sakshi, 'Stop asking and start doing roman Jaan.' Finally we enjoyed a lot of feelings on that night in our chat. That night, I quit my every shyness. I really love her. Now she is my wife. I was having my life's first roman with my wife only though in chat. I love you Sakshi. From the very next day, we talk like naughty couples sometimes. 8th December. I love this night. We had roman chat 2nd time on the New Year, as it was our first anniversary. But still we did roman only on chat, not physically. But still we feel quite shy in front of each other.

CHAPTER EIGHT

True Love Won

It was finally the most awaited day of my life: Priya didi's wedding. Unfortunately, I missed my family trip to Kashmir to attend her wedding. But no-one can stop me from attending her wedding after all her wedding was my dream. I learned about true love from her life. Finally, how can I miss the winning happiness of that true love? I can't. I am sorry Mom and Dad. In the Sindhi community, the wedding occurs in the city where the boy stays.

The *baraat* comes from the boy's home to the marriage hall where girls and her family stay in that marriage hall. Krishna Jiju belongs to Bombay, so I was invited by Priya di in the evening functions too, and then late at night, they had booked one bus in which we all are going from Palanpur to Bombay. Almost in every wedding, traveling takes place at night itself. The majority depends on the timing of marriage and its *rasams* [tradition]. My parents went for the trip, and as soon as I reached near Priya di's home, I don't know, but I was feeling a little nervous. Maybe as I was attending a wedding without my Mom and Dad for the first time. But luckily on the way, I saw Sakshi. Yes, I knew, even her Jiju had come to her home, so she was with her family. She didn't see me, but I did. I felt good after watching my future wife. For a moment I imagined her with me, instead of her sister and her jiju. Finally, I entered the building of Priya di's home. The function was on the first floor. Priya di saw me as I entered but as she was busy doing a puja or any other *rasam*, she just passed a smile. Priya di's father welcomed me and invited me inside. I refused and told him that I was waiting for Kruti ma'am. Actually, inside some ladies *rasam* (maybe Ladies Sangeet) was going on, so I didn't prefer to go without Kruti ma'am. After some time, Kruti ma'am entered, but as Priya di's parents knew her very well, she couldn't stop herself from going inside. With her eyes she asked me to join, but in response I said that it would be fine waiting here. I would love to see all traditions of a Sindhi wedding. Finally, Panditji completed the puja, and announced, 'Tonight, anyone who takes blessings from the bride will surely be granted every wish of theirs.' A very long smile occurred on my face hearing such words. Priya di and Kruti ma'am went inside the room, I insisted Priya Di's brother and father to give me some work, but they both were not ready to assign me any work as I was a guest for them. I tried to convince them, but both were not ready to budge. Finally, one little girl came and asked me, 'Are you Malav?'

I said, 'Yes.'

She informed me that Priya di was calling me inside the room. I went and saw her. She smiled and added, 'I know you will not enter my room by yourself.'

I replied, 'Di, anyway how's Jiju?'

'You are always flatter of your brother in law, have you asked how I am?' I smiled.

She added, 'I know you want to be an obedient brother-in-law. He is fine and happy too.'

I added, 'He will be happier than you.' Kruti ma'am joined in, 'But less than you. You seem to be the happiest person in this wedding.'

I smiled.

Kruti ma'am, 'My God, Priya just sees his face. Blushing! Every sister must have a brother like you.'

Priya di, 'Kruti, I am going to kill you, if you ever say like this. Touch-wood my brother.'

After a pause of 2 minutes, Priya di said, 'Don't you need my blessings tonight?'

And at the same time I said, 'Didi, I need your blessings today also!'

Again the three of us burst out and I took blessings by bowing down to her feet. She by keeping her left hand on my right cheeks said, 'God bless you. Love you.' Priya di's elder sister and her sister-in-law came to call her for dinner. In eye contact, Priya di invited me also, but I too responded to her to go, would join later. Both Priya di and Kruti ma'am went, and within a minute, Kruti ma'am came back and said, 'Your sister is not going to eat anything without you. So, will you please come with me leaving this shyness behind?' Her words made me smile, and gave me the guts to join them.

Priya di, 'You have very shy nature Malav.'

Kruti ma'am, 'And due to your shy nature, neither will she eat, nor she will allow me to eat. Don't mind I am very hungry.'

Priya di, 'Malav, I know you will keep silent and will not eat anything but will not leave your shyness. That's better you dine with me only.'

I smiled.

Kruti ma'am said, 'Listen Malav, it's Priya's wedding. She has a lot of responsibilities and a lot of tension in her mind. So, you must take care of yourself.'

I replied, 'Sure ma'am. Priya di, you don't need to worry for me at all.'

Kruti ma'am, 'Now happy Priya? And even I am there to take care of your brother. You just enjoy your every moment.'

Priya di, 'Ha baba, but Malav, you have to sit in the same bus, in which I sit tonight.'

By listening to such words Kruti ma'am, 'Hey Bhagwan. Again worry.'

I replied, 'Will try Priya di.'

Priya di, 'No, not only try, you have to.'

'But how will I ask in front of everyone.'

'That I don't know.'

Kruti ma'am interrupted us, 'Please brother and sister, eat your dinner fast. Then continue your love on the bus. I will bring you both on the same bus.' Finally, we completed our dinner.

Then Kruti ma'am and Priya di went to complete some work. Everybody was busy, so I got a chance to serve dinner to the guests. So, I started to serve dinner to every guest. I would love to serve in the homes where weddings take place. After every guest had completed dinner, Priya di's elder sister came towards me, and said in front of everyone, 'Malav, you had served in the home where the wedding is taking place, so Godji will surely give you a nice wife.'

I smiled and with little guts, I replied, 'Didi, I did all this not for gaining a nice wife, I did because I love to help and to work.' Everybody burst out with laughter.

This made me realise that in that whole room, only ladies were present. Their laughter made me feel shy, so I ran out of the room. Priya di's elder sister came outside the room and said, 'Priya was right. You are too innocent and pure of heart. God bless you.'

'Thank you di.' I bowed down to touch her feet.

'I know you had missed your family trip for attending Priya's wedding. She means a lot to you, right?'

I smiled and responded positively. Her didi also rotated her left hand on my cheeks. I felt too good. And yes, just for a moment, but when she said about my wife, Sakshi's face came to my mind. Anyway, afterwards I made Arti talk with Priya di, as she was in Chennai wasn't not able to come, due to her exams.

#

Finally, the time for traveling came. There were 2 mini-buses. Initially, I helped to shift luggage from the house to the bus, then elders ordered ladies to go on a small bus, only 2 to 3 gents, and all other gents on a large bus, as the number of gents' were more. So, I needed to wait for my turn, but Priya di called me and asked her father to send me on that small bus. I went inside, she made space for me in the first row, and Priya di was sitting on the second row, diagonal to me. In Sindhi weddings, every relative treats himself a lot. When I entered in the bus, everyone was watching me carefully because I was the one whom Priya di had proudly called from inside the bus. After 2 minutes, Priya Di's mom entered in the bus, but it was full, and as I said before, no relative was ready to give her space, but I stood without noticing that other people are trying to give their seat or not because I must give her my seat as it was her daughter's marriage. But even she refused to take my seat, I insisted that I will sit on another bus, but she said, 'You especially came for her. You sit here only; I will arrange myself on another bus.'

But finally, one of her relatives became ready to shift to another bus. Thank God, else I would have considered myself responsible to separate a daughter from her mother that too night before her marriage. The moment came where I get a chance to take care of the bride. Cold winds were blowing from the window of the bus, and Priya di was sitting on the second row, keeping her legs on my chair near my right hand. So, I kept my jacket over her legs, so she doesn't feel cold. She passed a smile, I felt too good. I cherish the moments I spent with her.

After some time, we stopped for a tea break around 4 o'clock, where she said, 'Don't care for me so much dear.'

I replied, 'What can I do? You know I love you a lot.'

'Idiot I love you too.'

Afterwards, Priya di's brother arranged 3 to 4 seats in a row for her so she could sleep well, and I shifted to her place, so Kruti ma'am slept on my shoulder, and I enjoyed the fresh morning cold air blowing near my window. Kruti ma'am was woken up by me when we reached the hotel. We all got ready one by one, as inside the city we were new, so we got a little late. So, in our case, the baraat reached before the relatives from the girl side had reached. But then too, we welcomed the whole family of the groom. Finally, the ceremony of Priya di's wedding began. Krishna Jiju entered the hall, one of Priya di's cousins washed his legs with milk. Kruti ma'am took Jiju's shoes. Afterwards the 7 rounds (*Saat phere*) started. I was watching every moment of her wedding. I was feeling too good, and my idol was marrying her true love. My life's first true love was winning. I was enjoying it a lot. I saw Jiju making Priya di wear her mangal sutra. Then he put red sindoor on her head (maang). In between Kruti ma'am called me for lunch, but I refused as I was enjoying it all. So, she had it with one another sir who had come to attend Priya di's wedding from our classes only. Then a moment came, where Priya di's father called me and asked me to become a part of the tradition. I was overwhelmed. Actually, Priya di did not have any real uncle, so Priya di's father asked me to be her uncle. I nodded but was too frightened, as I did not know what I had to do in this tradition. I asked her dad, her dad said, 'Don't worry, Panditji will guide you.' I had already kept 151 rupees in my upper pocket as I knew I have to donate it after each tradition. Panditji called me, I took out my shoes, so he washed my hands with pure water (water of Ganga River), then he told me to follow his mantras holding the hands of Priya di and Jiju.

I was very nervous, don't know why! But Panditji held my hand with their hands, Jiju in a slow voice said, 'Malav, why are you scared? Your di and I are with you only, so don't worry.' Such words generate a lot of confidence in me. Yes, I don't know which kind of fear I was having, but yes Jiju's words made my fears vanish.

I realised that I was feeling lucky to become part of my Priya di's wedding ceremonies though I was not her real brother. After this tradition, I donated 151 rupees in Panditji's pocket. Priya di's brother tried to give me that money from his pocket, but I refused. I really enjoyed the whole tradition. After completion of every tradition, there comes the time for the bride's farewell. I had already promised Priya di that I will take care of myself, so I decided and made myself so strong that at least I will not cry. But I was shocked when I saw Kruti ma'am even crying.

I tried to console her and said, 'Ma'am, don't cry. She is marrying the one whom she loves a lot.'

Kruti ma'am replied, 'Dear, now her responsibilities will increase. Now, she is no more in our city that we can meet anytime. Now she will not be able to talk much, and will not even be able to chat the whole day, because now her primary responsibility is towards her in-laws.'

Hearing such words made me a little weak, but I didn't allow a tear to enter my eyes and said to myself (my blue one), 'Krishna Jiju will take care of her at every moment. He will not make her feel our absence.'

I said to myself (my red one), 'But what if I will feel her absence.'

Again the blue one said, 'Idiot, she is marrying her true love. That's it.' Finally, I controlled myself.

#

We were back at the hotel, and everyone was not going to be ready for the reception. This time Priya di was not with us. We reached the hall, and I was shocked watching gorgeous Priya didi. She was wearing a saree which was red and Jiju was wearing a black suit with a red tie. They were looking like a Bollywood couple. In my imagination, both were looking like RadhaKrishna. Kruti ma'am and I went on stage to congratulate both of them. Afterwards, Kruti ma'am took me first for dinner, as she knew I didn't have my lunch. After dinner, photography began again with Priya di and Krishna Jiju. Finally, the wedding ceremonies were complete and we all were going back. So, every family member of Priya di again went on stage to say the last goodbye to Priya di. Everyone was crying again. Kruti ma'am, Priya di's elder sister, her mom, everybody was crying on stage. Even Priya di cried. I too feel a little low, so to control myself I didn't go above on stage.

Jiju called me to join them, but I refused, as it was making me feel weird if I would cry in front of her relatives because I was not her real brother. Hence, I joined my hands from there only and said *namaste* to Jiju. With my face, Jiju read what I want to say, that is, 'Please take care of my sister. *Bhul chuk maff karna* (Forgive me for any mistakes).'

Within a moment, Jiju's brother came and said, 'Don't worry, I and your Jiju will handle everything here, even my bhabhi.' I felt too good. He just met me once in the ring ceremony, but his time of saying such words make me feel too good for Priya di's in-laws. He understands my relationship with Priya di and my attachment towards her. I am thankful to Godji for giving such wonderful in-laws to Priya di. Then we were back to our city the next morning. Kruti ma'am, as usual, slept on my shoulder in the night. I enjoyed the ride on the window seat and on another shoulder my lovely Kruti ma'am.

Yes, it was the moment I missed my Sakshi. As soon as I reached home, I went to my college city as there was no one at my home. Finally, while catching the train for my college city, I called my Sakshi. I had not talked to her since the last two days. I called her and said, 'Dearji, 2 days gone? And you are not following your resolution?'

Actually, on 1st Jan, she had taken one resolution. According to that, she had to give me a kiss every morning. So, she replied, 'Dearji, you will surely get your part of the resolution, that too with interest. Don't worry, but do share your experience of attending the wedding. I am eagerly waiting to attend Priya di's wedding.'

'It's over, now how will you attend?'

'In your experience dearji, I know you will share with me like I will feel I am attending it.' So I shared my whole lovely experience with her.

And in return, she had given me a lot of kisses. Finally, I was back to my normal life. That is college going well. I had heard that the best gift is time, and my college friend Ishika's birthday was around the corner so I had time for her gift, that is I prepared a card for her birthday. On her birthday, I gave it to her and she felt good, though it was simple, but she felt it was sweet. Along with the card, I gave her a diary just like my personal diary to her. Because I think she will love to write a diary like me. Ankita, my study partner, and my friend shared about her love Ankit. Even in college, almost everyone knows about my relationship with Sakshi. But no-one really knew her. Instead of Sakshi, I had told them her name to be Bhumi, as I don't want to spoil a girl's name, till she got engaged to me. The second year was going to end, so in college, everyone liked to share their talks as almost everyone had a boyfriend or a girlfriend. Like we have one silent guy Pratik in our batch, he was also now my good friend, he also had a girlfriend Vaani, whom he loved from the school time, and she was ready to marry him whenever he would say. But he wanted to study first. Almost everyone was committed, or had a crush at least. I was very attached to everyone, so every friend had shared their personal life with me, and I had shared mine with everyone too. Sometimes my college friend used to call me Bhumi only in the lab. Anyways, life was going well and I was happy to see true love winning in every phase of life. As compared to yesterday, I am feeling more mature today.

CHAPTER NINE

Valentine Shocks

My life was going too well. Like everyone, I too expect fun, enjoyment, and love in my life without any problems. But as time passes, I feel more mature than yesterday. Sometimes in college life, I understand the moment, where I need to make some decisions. I have to select one among 2 people who are opposite to each other, but both are my friends. But life teaches us at every moment, all due to my Sakshi, my love. I have many friends, but I never get frightened to lose anyone, like I was in the past with Arti. Since, I was having my love at every step of my life. But unfortunately, this time also, on Valentine's Day I was not able to meet my Sakshi though it was on Sunday. Especially on this day, our parents have eyes on us. But at least I wish to spend some time with her. So, I know myself, that I don't need any preparation for making a romantic atmosphere because she knows that I am romantic. Every girl likes a romantic guy. But it was the great saying that 'Everything doesn't happen as we think'. I called her at midnight and said, 'Happy Valentine Day Jaan.'

She replied, 'Happy Valentine Dayyyy Muah'

I said, 'Oh ho, today I got my share of the resolution sooner than I had expected.'

She replied, 'I love you Jaan.

Today I too need my resolution'

I, 'Muah'

She, 'Only one?'

I replied, 'Muaaaaaah 😘 😘'

She lastly said, 'Ok Jaan, now let me wear your favourite night suit, that Gunjan wala (tv celebrity) used to wear Shirt and pyjama in night suit till the time Dad will sleep, and I already managed to sleep alone tonight, so give me 5 minutes.'

'Jaan, tonight also you will sleep.'

'No Jaan, I need to talk.'

'Only talk?'

'First only talk, then depends on you.'

'On me? You know what I want to do?'

'I know what you want to do. And even know what you will do.'

'The same thing dearji.'

'No dearji, though you want to do roman, you will not do it as far as I know you.'

'But why, tonight it's valentine's night, I wish to do roman, and you too wish the same I know. Then why will I change my mood? I am unable to understand what you are saying?'

'Jaan let me change and call you back.'

'Ok Jaan, wear my favourite night suit fast and keep its buttons loose. It makes it easy to open.'

'Jaan, please.'

'Ok baba, I am waiting.' We disconnected, and I prepared my bed for sleep, as I used to talk with her under a blanket, so no-one can hear my talks, but tonight, no-one is in my room, as some went home, some went with their girlfriends, and some with friends.

I was alone in my room. I prepared, and finally slept on the bed, and was waiting for her call. As time passed, I was wishing valentine to friends. Everyone was saying that they think I will be busy with my girlfriend. I replied that you can check my call after 10 minutes, it will be busy only. Finally, Sakshi gave me a missed call. I called her and asked her, 'Will you be my valentine?'

'I want to be your valentine, but before it, I want to give some shocks to you.'

'What shocks?'

'I mean I want to give you some shocking news.'

'What?'

'Dearji, I want to confess something, after which you might never talk with me again.'

'That's never going to happen. You say what you did.'

'You remember, Aashish?'

'Yes, the name you used to avoid me, and to avoid yourself for being attracted to me.'

'Yes, but it is not the only name. That person exists and even you know him. You used to play with him in childhood because his cousin lives in your society only. His name is Johnny.'

'Oh yes, that Aashish, Johnny's cousin, I remember that person with so much attitude.'

'Maybe he likes me.'

'But you don't like him; if he wants to be your friend, and you too want the same, then I don't have any problem dearji. I trust you dearji. You frighten me without any reason.'

'But now he is my brother, but then too he wants me as her girlfriend.'

'What? Tell me clearly what you want to say.'

'Okay ji, I am saying this with a lot of guts, so please don't say anything still I complete.'

'Okay, I promise.'

Sakshi started to say, 'Till grade X you know, I was too shy. I don't even see towards any boy except you, as you were my crush that too I am realising now when I became mature. And you know Raju, my cousin's brother studies in our class itself. And you also know how he was, so in school, if any boy used to talk with me, he used to beat him. Once he had fought with our classmate Chirag and I came to know this after 2 years. Chirag was beaten by Raju because Chirag told some of his friends that he likes me. So, I know he was my protective brother, till X. But as our school becomes different after X, so when I used to go tuitions in 11th on my vehicle. After a few days, I realised that Aashish is following me every day. I avoided it for some days, but one day he came toward me and directly proposed to me.'

I was shocked. I asked him, 'Who are you?'

He replied, 'I am Aashish. I am your neighbour.'

I didn't reply to him. But on the second day, again he proposed to me.

I said, 'No.'

But again for some days continuously he came towards me and proposed to me.

Finally, after a week I replied, 'If you want to become a friend then its fine.' I thought, at least he will stop following me.

But he replied, 'No, I love you. I want to marry you only.' I replied, 'If you live in my neighbourhood, then you must know our family. They are not going to accept a love marriage.'

He replied, 'That I will manage. You just say once that you love me.'

I denied his request and left him. He tried to force me almost every day. After a month, he called me and said, 'Sakshi, I am at the bridge, and going to commit suicide, if you don't come here within 5 minutes.'

So I panicked and went to save him. To save him I had to accept his proposal. Hence, slowly we became close to each other.

I asked her, 'You mean to say, whatever you were telling me initially was the truth. It means, even he kissed you. Whatever we talked about that he kissed you on your cheeks in the garden was all truth. Right?'

Sakshi replied, 'Yes, but I had no other option.'

'What do you mean by that you have no other option? He kissed you on your cheeks! You had an affair with him.'

'I mean, I was not having any option at the time of his proposal, but after I accepted his proposal, I even felt attraction towards him.'

'But why did you hide it from me?' The first time, tears came to my eyes so fast.

She realised it and said, 'Jaan, please don't cry. I was confused; I was unable to understand at that time, and even now, because I was frightened that I might lose you. Please Jaan, let me complete the whole past, don't give any such reactions which make me stop. Please it's a request that you think like this that I am telling you the truth.'

'Okay, go ahead, what happened next? How did you both break up? And what is this brother matter? And yes, how many times have you gone on a date with him? And how many times has he kissed you. I want to know everything. Tell me the whole thing; don't hide anything from me please. Okay?'

She continued, 'Then, slowly we become close. He used to come to meet me after my chemistry class. Not daily, but twice in a week. And we just once went to a garden where he kissed on my cheeks. Please don't cry. Other than this, once I went on a long drive with him in his car on the front seat. I am sorry. Please stop crying. I am feeling bad. In this world, we are the first, whom the boy is crying, and the girl used to console a boy.'

'Are we a couple?'

'Please don't say like this. I used to say tell him that our family will never be ready for us, but he always says that he will manage.'

'And you believed him, right?'

'Maybe yes. Once her mother came to know about our relationship, so she called me in the absence of Aashish and asked me about my relationship with him.'

I replied to her, 'Have you not asked this question to your son?'

Ashish's mother tried to show me the fear of my parents and said, 'If I inform your dad, then your dad will never allow you to go outside your home. Your studies, going out with your friends everything will get restricted. So, I am warning you to stop all this nonsense.'

I replied to her, 'Why don't you tell all this to your son? He went to the bridge for committing suicide.'

His mother said in a lower voice than before said, 'Dear, I will tell him too, but please stop all this. From now onwards, he will not disturb you.' Sakshi to me , "From that day, whenever her mom saw me, she used to show me her eyes. Initially, I avoided her, but then I used to show her my eyes too, after all, it was not my mistake. After all this, on the day of Rakhi, I went to his home, and tied him Rakhi.'

I asked, 'And he allowed you to do the same?'

Sakshi replied, 'How will he not allow me when his mom was standing in front of us. I already told him that our family will not be ready. From that day, I talk with him like a brother itself.'

'Sakshi, do you think relationships are games? Whenever love fails, brother sister exists. This is the greatest problem of the current generation. He still loves you, and if you don't love him, then why are you in contact with him till now?'

'I never loved him; I just had an attraction towards him. And trust me Malav. I treat him only as my brother.'

'Ok I trust you. Just answer one question honestly. 'You treated him like your brother, but did he treat you as a sister?"

She became silent for a moment and said,'I don't know. Sometimes, he talks like a sibling, and sometimes like that… depends on his mood.'

'Oh, now I came to know why you told me the truth tonight. That depends on his mood, it means tonight he has wished you for Valentine's Day, Am I right?'

She replied in affirmation and added, 'But I didn't reply to him.'

But I was unable to tolerate it at that moment, so in anger, I disconnected her call. It was our first fight. I switched my cell phone off. My eyes had tears in them. I was confused. There was no-one in my room. Her words were repeating in my mind. There arose a sharp pain in my heart. She had cheated on me. As soon as the word cheat came into my mind, I realised if she wanted to cheat, then she would have hidden it tonight as well. If I react like this, she will never tell the truth which will hurt me. So, I switched the phone on. Her message was there,'Jaan, please I am worried. Talk to me. Please it's a request that doesn't do anything which hurts you and me and every one of your family. Please don't do anything wrong. Trust me Jaan, you are my hubby. Right? Please I am sorry.'

Reading her message, I realised, she still loves me. So, there was no question of cheating. She cares for me. Maybe I need some time to understand what happened between us. Because I know many times situations create misunderstandings. So, I called her, 'Hello.'

She asked, 'Are you ok? I am so sorry.'

'Don't worry, I am not like him and will not do anything which affects my parents. Godji has given such a beautiful life. So, what if there are problems, I don't believe in attempting suicide. And yes, don't be sorry. I think it's just a situation that is playing a great role in our life. I need time to understand your shock, Shona. I need time.'

'Sure Jaan, but you know, I always wished that you would call me Shona, and this is the first time you called me but see the time.'

'You sleep. Good night.'

'You too don't think much. Sleep soon. Guddy night. Love you.'

After ending our call, it was 2:00 AM on 14 February. She slept even without noticing that I didn't say guddy today. She told guddy, but I used to say guddy only to her, and Priya di, that too because guddy is written by me when I am in a good mood. She said once that I used to write daily, but in actual I used to write only when I was happy, every day I was with Sakshi, so I was happy. But today my heart didn't feel so guddy. Anyways, my brain was having many thoughts playing kabaddi.I think my mind will burst soon. I love her and she loves me too. She is loyal also, hence she told me the truth, but what is she doing at present with him. Actually, I know how boys are, but please Malav, try to understand yourself. You just need to think about Sakshi. She treats him only as a brother. And whatever happened, it was in the past. She has no other option to save him. And when I realise that I was immature yesterday, then why she can't. She was immature at that time. It is obvious when we spend time with someone, we feel attracted, then attachment increases, and hence feelings. But if she has feelings of love for him, then till today she had loved him only, but she was in love with me today. Hence, she told the truth. She was not wrong in the past or in the present. It was just that circumstances came in such a bad way that she got proved wrong in front of me. If she had told the truth after marriage, then I would have gotten more hurt and what if Aashish in future said that I have used a girl. Instead, I must respect Sakshi for telling me the truth. She had gathered guts for it. I have pain in my heart, though I got hurt, but the truth is that pain can be healed by her only with time. I love her. And remember Malav, she is just yours at present and will be only yours in the future too. Finally, this whole thought process took me 2 hours. I slept at 4 and I already decided that I will behave normally with her as her hubby itself.

#

Sakshi texted me at 8, I needed to reply but I don't know what stopped me to reply. She again texted me, 'Don't you need your resolution on this auspicious day?'

Finally, I replied, 'Obviously I need.'

She texted me 7 kisses. (7 & 2 are my lucky numbers).

After 5 minutes, she again texted me, 'Sometimes, I too need something in return for following my resolution.'

In my frustration I replied, 'Go and ask for it from your Aashish na?'

She called me and politely said, 'On Valentine's day, a girl needs a kiss from her hubby, not from brother.'

I replied, 'Don't you dare to talk with me so sweetly. It will not decrease my anger.'

'Your anger is right. Shout me, scold me still you want, I will not say a single word in reply. You are my hubby and you have the right to scold me. But the truth is we both love each other till now.'

My voice became low, I said, 'Jaan, you were right. If you had informed me about it earlier, maybe I was unable to understand it, might you have lost me. I don't know, but in my heart I am feeling proud of you dearji. Whatever you did, you have believed in yourself that you are right in confessing. Always believe in yourself.'

'I have learned all this from you only Malavji.'

'Love you Sakshi.'

'Love you Aeydha.'

'Hey, it's my favourite.'

'Yes, for my favourite, his favourite word from my side.' We decided on how to handle this matter. She said, 'Now I will tell him clearly, and if required I will tell him that I love someone else. After it also, if he will not agree then I will do whatever you will say.'

'He is your past, so I know you can handle him. Do whatever you feel right, in the end, I am always there for you. Lastly, I will handle him in boys' way.'

'Thank you, Jaan and Sorry too.'

'Don't be Jaan. You were right in the past. You saved him. You are right in the present too. You were not mature in the past at that age. But as soon as you realised, you told the truth to me, so I am happy with you, and your decision. I love you forever.'

As it was Sunday, her dad was at home, so she couldn't talk on the phone much; we were only chatting. I slept at noon, as I didn't properly sleep at night. I called Arti in the evening to wish her Valentine, but she was busy with her new boyfriend. Yes, she finally moved on, and now in college, she fell in love with Kishen. I didn't stop myself from calling my Sakshi.

I said, 'Hi Sakshi, what's up?'

'Nothing much, going to the temple.'

'Why? On Valentine's day, you gave me such shock, so going to say sorry to Godji.' I didn't realize but I was taunting her.

'No, I am going to thank Godji for making you so strong that you tolerate my shock and even forgave me after it.'

'Jaan, forget it.'

'These words, I should say to you. I hurt you. Anyway, can we continue after coming back from the temple?'

'You are taking too much time once you go to the temple. It's my daily experience. You go there everyday I know and come back late.'

'No, no dear, I am going to the temple, not to the ashram. Daily I go to the ashram, from where I come late, but today I am going to Lord Jhulelal temple.'

'Why are you not going to the ashram today when you go there every day?'

'I will never go there from today.'

'Why?'

'I will tell you after coming back. I am getting late.'

'Ok dearji, go.'

But she didn't call until it was night. I was waiting, so her text came, 'Dearji, it is Sunday, Dad at home only, so unable to call you, but don't worry I am arranging for tonight's talk. Call you soon at night. Be ready.' I understand what she meant by the sentence, 'Be ready.' It indicates our last night's dream of roman.

Valentine Roman. This time, I need to prepare my heart, because inside my heart, still it was having little pain. She gave me a missed call at 11 o'clock. I too arranged the bed like yesterday. It was the same as no one was in the room today as well and I went under the blanket. And finally, I called her at 11:15 PM.

I said, 'Jaan, I wish you again, Happy Valentine Day. Will you be my valentine?'

She replied, 'Today I gave you a shock, then too you are ready to accept me. You are such a darling.'

'Dear forget whatever we discussed last night.'

'How can I forget dearji? As still, one more shock is remaining. I need to give it to you.'

I thought she was kidding. So, in reply, I said, 'Why? What happened now? Had Aashish kissed you on your lips too?'

'Not Aashish. But what if anyone else did?'

Her voice informed me that she is serious. She was right, hearing her words, I was really shocked. There was a lot of anger in my body, my mind wanted to burst out, my heart wanted to choose death rather than tolerating such pain. I was expecting Valentine Roman from the previous night, but her shocks are not ending.

I asked, 'Who?'

'Today evening I said that I will tell you why I don't want to go to the Ashram. It's because of Aakash Bhaiya.'

I angrily shouted at her, 'Are you out of your mind?'

'Please don't shout. Calm down. First, listen to the whole matter.'

'Why should I not shout? He is your brother. You always said he is your brother. Even now when you informed his name, you added bhaiya at the end. He is the helper (*sevadari*) at Ashram. He is Brahmachari.'

'Yes, I know dear, please dearji calm down, else I would be unable to say. Your loud voice scares me and my heart starts to cry which makes me lose my guts. Please I am informing you after gathering a lot of guts. Let me complete.'

For her, I controlled my anger and said to her, 'Ok, I am not shouting. Continue.'

'Aakash Bhaiya is Ashram's *sevadari*, but many girls come to help him to take care of the Ashram. I used to go on vacation. He used to hug each and every woman and girl whenever he met. And it's our family heritage to go to Ashram and do help (*seva*). My grandmother, my mother, my sister, and I all used to go there for help. But in the last vacation, I saw him going with a girl in the bathroom for more than an hour. When she came out, she was laughing. The next day I saw him again but with another girl. When she came out, she was also laughing.'

'Bullshit Man. He was using them.'

'I felt too awkward watching this. But I ignored it. But once at noon, I went to help him, so he hugged me initially, then he took me in a room behind the ashram and told me to clean up that room as some guests were going to come there to stay. He ordered me the instructions and I was following it. But in ordering me, he came towards me and within a minute he kissed my lips. I was unable to understand what was happening.'

'Idiot, why didn't you push him?'

'I couldn't because he was much older and stronger than me. After a moment he left my lips, asked me how I felt. But I didn't reply and came out of the room. I was confused on that day. I thought about sharing it with someone, but I know no-one will believe me, as he is a great sevadari, so I was afraid that everyone would tell me only.'

'But at least you had to inform your mom.'

'I tried dearji. I told mom that he used to hug me every time that I don't like it. But mom replied to me that he used to do that with everyone. He is a Brahmachari. So, don't you dare to think any bad about him. He has been doing God's service for too many years. By her words, I didn't have guts to say further about the kiss to her. Mom just ordered me to go to the ashram on vacation to help. The next day, again he took me in that room and kissed me again on my lips. That whole week he did the same. One day, he called me and ordered me to clean the bathroom, and took me to show it. I followed him. As soon as we reached, he pushed me inside and locked the door.'

'Sakshi, you are... I don't have words for you, for your stupidity. Anyways what happened next?' I realized my eyes already started to become wet.

'He took out my dupatta, holding my hands straight to the wall and came forward to kiss my lips. But I turned my face so he kissed on my cheeks. Then he asked me, 'What happened? Don't you like this?' This time I said a straight 'no'. He asked,'Should I leave your hands?''

I nodded yes. He left, I took my dupatta, opened the door, and left the ashram.'

'Idiot, you must have slapped him.'

'But I was confused as to whatever he was doing; I was not able to understand. At that moment, I did not know what to do, even I did not know that whatever is happening was right or wrong. From that day, I used to avoid going to the Ashram. Before some time, I heard that one whole night, one girl was with him at ashram due to rain outside, so...'

She paused, I completed, 'So they had sex. Right ?'

'People used to say it, but no-one had ever complained against him. That girl got married soon. And you know, the person whom she got married to is my far relative, who used to come to my home frequently. Even I had informed you earlier about that relative.'

'Yes, that one who came to prepare songs' CD on your PC, right?'

'Yes. Once he was sad and he shared that he is going to divorce his wife as she was already pregnant. He told me that I am ready to accept her child but she was not ready to accept her mistake. We got married 6 months earlier but she is pregnant for 8 months. I didn't inform him, but inside I knew that his wife is the same girl who spent the night with Aakash Bhaiya. Because I was not sure, maybe they were rumours and it was none of my business.'

'I think you are the world's greatest idiot. But I don't know why everyone used to share their personal life with you only.'

'I am sorry dearji. Initially, I was confused, but when I realised I stopped him. And now I am avoiding him.'

'Okay, I understand that he took advantage of innocent little girls who are immature. Not women, he is doing it with girls, because he knows which girls are still virgins.I have a question, he was kissing you for one whole week. But when he went one step ahead, how did you realise that it was wrong?'

'Due to you dearji. Because on that morning, you told me that roman after marriage occurs only between a hubby and his wife. So, I realised whatever he is doing with me, was not his right. It was only yours.'

I was shocked and shouted loudly, 'What? This is not your past. This all happened when you were in a relationship with me. It means you cheated me.'

'No dearji, it was just 4 to 5 months of our commitment. We were new in our relationship and not so close to talk like that. But on that day, the first time you said those words and I realised. I told you last vacation.'

'But at that time, you were not a child. I thought he used to do this only to childish immature girls. How can you do that to me? When I proposed to you, and you accepted, from that moment, you became mine, I believe we were one, not two. But you don't have such knowledge either. Instead of you, if any 5-year-old girl was present and any boy tries to kiss that she also starts to cry, and you were in a relationship, then too was not able to understand when he was kissing. Instead, you allowed him to continue for 7 days. If I had not talked about it on that morning, then might be you would have had sex with him, right?'

Sakshi, 'Malav, don't talk like that about your wife. I am sorry.'

Malav, 'Sakshi, you don't have a brain. Whatever I told it was a bitter truth. How can you be so simple, innocent, and lack awareness about boy's bad wishes (*buri nazare*)? How can you expect me now your hubby?'

I cried. My eyes were full of tears. I added, 'Sakshi, suppose in future as your husband if I want to kiss you on your lips, how can I? Because whenever I hear the words 'kiss' and 'lips' I imagine him kissing you and you are not stopping him. This is unbelievable Sakshi. I don't know but at present, I don't want to talk with you.' I disconnected the call.

I saw the time. Valentine's Day was already over. I saluted my love. I was laughing at myself. I shouted in the sky. Well done God in creating such a beautiful love story. Just a day before this I was feeling different about my life and my love story. And within a day, my feelings have changed drastically. Obviously, every lover feels the change in their life after this day and before this day. But after this day, every lover feels very happy, I am the only one who is feeling bad on and after this day. I don't know about Sakshi currently. I don't want to think about her at present. She gave me two beautiful shocks as a valentine's gift. Her first shock I can understand that it was her past. But, what about the second? It was not past. She cheated on me. I cried for the whole night. I tried to stop my tears, but her words were in my mind, the heart was paining more than yesterday night, so tears were not ready to stop. I don't know whether I had loved the one who is so innocent that she doesn't care about such things, or I had loved who can use and throw me. I don't know what to do. Too many bad thoughts are coming to my mind. I thought to share it with someone, but I can't call Priya di, because she was busy in her married life. I can't call anyone late at night.

I called Arti, but her line was busy, I understood she must be talking to Kishen. Then I thought, I can't share this with Arti, because suppose if in future I would like to be with Sakshi, then Arti will see her with different eyes. No-one will understand Sakshi like I do. So, I decided that I cannot share it with anyone. I have to decide alone. Nobody will support me to accept Sakshi, Everyone will call me mad. I am thinking about all this as I have just a point in my mind that she is loyal to me. But she cheated on me unintentionally, this was also the truth. Aashish and Aakash Bhaiya, Godji will not forgive you both for spoiling my life. She allowed him to kiss her on her lips continuously for 7 days. I cried a lot. I felt I lost in my love story. The whole night, I just cried. There were 17 missed calls from Sakshi, but I didn't receive a single one. There were too many messages, but I deleted them without reading. I needed time. This was the first time I slept without wiping my tears.

\#

On 15 February, Sakshi woke me up in the morning by calling, but I disconnected her call. I went to college, but in my mind, still I was confused. I ignored everyone in college for the whole day. I was angry at Sakshi, and I don't want to take out my anger on anyone else. So, nobody was with me on that day. I was feeling very bad. At the end of college, I was going alone back to my room. My friends had already gone as I told them that I am had some work in college. While going back, I thought of calling Sakshi, but again what would I say to her. I agree she is loyal as she told the truth, but whatever she did hurt me. So, I still can't talk, I don't decide what to do about our relationship. I have to decide alone. I need help, I need a suggestion, but it is also the fact that no-one will understand her like I do. Because I know her, no-one else knows her like I do. But how can I decide alone since I have a lot of frustration left inside me?

I want to take out that first. Finally, I shouted a little to Godji, 'Hey Bhagwan, I always believe that in one or the other way, you are giving any kind of signal whenever I need it. So please show me the correct path. Please.'

Some voice replied to my sentence, 'Right from the next pillar.'

I was shocked and turned back. It was Ishika who replied. She saw me and laughed loudly.

After completion of her laughter, what you thought, 'For you, *Aakashvani hui* (oracle happens). I am sorry. A right turn from the next pillar will make you reach your room. And it's the correct path.' She again laughed.

For a moment, I forgot my problems and was enjoying watching her laughing face. Soon I realised my problems again and as I decided I have to hide it from everyone, so I made myself normal.

I asked her, 'Why? You are coming so late from college.'

She replied, 'Because your Godji sent me. Ha ha ha.'

Again she started laughing.

After 2 minutes, she controlled her laughter and said, 'Actually I went to meet my friend in the girls' hostel. So, I am coming back now. I am sorry for my laughter, but I can't control it once it starts. By the way, it's nice to know that I am not the only one who talks to herself on the way. I have been watching you since the last 5 minutes. You were not only talking but doing actions while talking same as me. And I really enjoyed it.'

I replied, 'No you have a habit of doing it. And I did the first time that too you interrupted.'

She replied, 'Oh really, whatever, I really enjoyed it.' A cute smile was still on her face. I showed her expressions by showing her half tongue. She again started to laugh and continued to laugh for 5 min.

Finally, I said, 'Enough Ishika, how much you will laugh? Your stomach will pain.'

She replied in laughter, 'It's already paining.'

Finally, she controlled and drank water. We stopped for a moment. I asked her, 'You seem to be happy, anything special.'

'Yes, I met my best friend after a lot of time.'

'Oh ho, who is that lucky person?'

'Vishaka, she lives in a hostel and studies Pharmacy.'

'Oh, nice.'

She asked, 'By the way, how was your valentine's day?'

I said to myself with an inner voice, 'What should I say to her now? Shall I share with her? Maybe she can help me.'

I replied to her, 'Nice.'

She replied, 'No, I want to know in detail. How did you feel? What did you give her, and what she gifted you? Listen Malav, I am comfortable with you only about such talks. Though I know you are shy, but you are the only one who trusted me and informed me about your lover.'

I replied, 'Ok.'

She interrupted, 'Friend, can't we talk peacefully? If you don't mind, let's first go to our rooms, and get fresh, then meet for a walk and will talk.'

I replied, 'Yes sure, it's a lot of time that we were not gone for a walk.'

She smiled. I added, 'I am going on a walk only with you.'

'Same here Malav.'

'Ok, but I would share with you only on one condition.'

'Which condition?'

'I want your suggestion in one matter. So, you have to help me with that.'

'Sure.'

'Okay, see you then.'

I came to the room and thought again, 'Should I share it with Ishika? What would she think of Sakshi then? I mean Bhumi. What if she would tell everyone in college? No, no, I can trust her. This is my personal matter; she will not share with anyone. But what will happen if she meets Sakshi in the future? Like I feel now that she cheated me, like in my imagination I have a situation that Aakash is kissing her. What if she feels the same, and if she has such imagination? She might see her differently. No, I don't think it's appropriate to share with her. I can trust her, but Sakshi will not like it if such talk I will share with someone else. But Malav, you are still thinking about Sakshi. She cheated on you. And you are sharing because you need a suggestion. You are sharing with your friend only, not with any elder. She understands. I am confused again. Anyway, let's see. Most probably I am not going to share with her. I will divert my mind and want to feel relaxed. So, I am going with one nice friend on a walk in the fresh evening air.'

I reached near her hostel and as usual, she was waiting. This time she was too eager to know about my valentine's day like once upon a time, I was eager to know about the love story of my Priya di. She said, 'I am waiting for you to start.'

I started to make a story, 'First she called and wished me then I did some general talks.'

She said with sad expressions, 'That's it.'

I replied, 'Yes, I already said it's not a story, friend.'

'Okay now tell me the matter in which I have to give a suggestion.'

'No, it's fine, I got the solution.'

We almost completed one round in which I didn't say much. And in actual I was avoiding talking because I was still confused and sad. But I don't know when we completed the first round and started the second round of walking. My heart was feeling danger, pain, I tried to enjoy the fresh air and a nice friend but failed. She even got it.

So, she asked, 'Malav, any problem?'

I replied to her negatively. She said, 'Malav, I can read your expressions. Don't hide forcefully, or don't act normal if you aren't, because you don't know how to lie.'

Finally, I decided to share with her, but indirectly, after all, I want to find out some solution. It's my life, a great matter in which I can get help only from best friends.

I replied, 'Actually I am still worried about that matter.'

She said, 'I knew it. You still didn't get a solution, you just avoided initially. Might be such a matter was complicated to share. Malav, believe me, sharing helps to feel us good. Trust me. And if you are comfortable with me, then I am always with you.'

I said, 'I trust you a lot. Actually, the matter is about my friend's personal life, so...'

Ishika replied, 'Okay, then it's up to you whether you want to share or not.'

I said, 'Yes, Okay, I am telling but please don't tell anyone. I hope you understand. My friend loves a girl who made a mistake. Now she confessed her mistake in front of my friend. Now, he is confused and needs my help, but after listening to her whole matter, I am even confused. I am sharing, because you are a girl, you might understand in a better way.'

She said, 'Ok, then tell me the matter. Don't talk extra. I can understand Malav.'

I replied, 'Ok, Listen. Actually, that mistake is that girl was kissed by someone else that too on lips.'

'Forcefully?'

'No.'

'Then your friend must slap her. For every girl, lip kisses are a great feeling.'

Listening to her harsh words for my Sakshi made me angrier, especially the word, 'slap'.

But I controlled myself, and I shouted slowly, decreasing my voice, 'First listen to the whole matter dear. She was small when he kissed her. And the person who kissed her was her family friend.'

She replied, 'Thank God, then it's a different matter. Sorry, I reacted too fast. I don't allow my friend to have such a girlfriend, sorry special friend. For a moment I thought it was my friend so I reacted too fast. Sorry.'

'It's fine.'

'Ok, then what is the problem?'

'That boy was her family friend, so he is still trying on her for some time. And her family relations are so strong, that her mother doesn't trust her. So, she can't avoid maintaining relations with him. A formal relation with him gives too much pain to my friend. So, what is to be done?'

'First thing, every mother trusts her daughter a lot, but maybe she felt ashamed or panicked, so she did not tell her the whole truth. The more important thing is that if your friend truly loves her, then he has to support her. Also, he needs to sacrifice his pain because I think girls feel more pain. She hates him, but still necessary for her to keep relation with him. So think from how much pain she might suffer?'

'Yes, I am thinking the same. If she had wanted to cheat, then she wouldn't have informed *me* herself.'

She shocked and stopped, and turned her face towards me. I was caught by the word 'me'.

I confessed, 'Yes, it is me only. And this is about Bhumi only.'

'Yes, I have a doubt since you were affected too much when I said slap her.'

'Yes, but I don't know why I lied to you though you helped me a lot. Thanks. And I am so sorry...'

'Listen, friend. I can understand. Our second round of walk was just for your problem.'

Oh, I noticed that the first round was already completed.

I replied, 'Thanks a lot.'

'Don't be. I just pushed you, but you already had decided what you want to do. You love her too much, and I am too happy about it. You just need a little push which I gave. I am sorry because unintentionally I hurt you by asking you questions about your valentine's day. I did not know that it was not a good day for you.'

'No, it's not your mistake.'

'Okay, then go back to the room, and tell her loudly that you still love her.'

'Okay, but please in college...'

'Malav, even I forget what you shared. By sharing such matters, you showed a great amount of trust in me. I will never break it.'

'Yes, you understand. Can you do one more favour?'

'Yes, Sure.'

'Ishika, I don't know how to say this, but Bhumi was so small when this happened... I mean she did not know about it at that time... So ... She told the truth by herself.'

'Malav, relax. Neither you nor her impression has decreased in my eyes. Instead, it increases. I am proud of you friend and your love. I respect you both more than initially because she told the truth and anyhow you don't want to leave her hand.'

I don't know how to thank God and her. God sent her at the perfect time. And she helped me a lot. She understood everything, my confusion, my feeling; though I lied to her that Sakshi was a child. But then too indirectly she made me realise what I want. Yes, she was right, I was just in need of little push, which she gave, I need Sakshi. I turned towards my room and said bye to her. Just a moment later my hand touched my pocket, so I again turned back and called loudly, 'Ishika.'

She turned her face and I saw her earrings. I realised it was the same which I saw in college on the first day in Lecture Hall. It means it was she who was sitting on the second last row. She reached towards me and asked, 'What happened again?'

'Yes, you want to know what I am going to gift her.'

'Yes.'

I took out a box from my pocket. It contained an anklet. I showed her.

Ishika, 'Oh so nice Malav. It is the best gift ever for a girl from her boyfriend on Valentine's Day. Lucky Girl.'

'Thank you. I hope she even likes it.'

'Malav, as a friend, I was worried for you because I know you are too innocent. But I trust your trust and love. So, go and tell her that you still love her. I am sure she will like this too much.'

Finally, I reached the room.

#

I called Sakshi and informed her that I am coming home on the 17th and want to meet you on the 18th. She replied, 'I will be glad to meet you.'

'Do not think that everything is patched up, I can stay upset with you for the entire life on this topic, and can also keep taunting you for the same. Is it alright?'

'Ok dearji, you don't know how relaxed I am feeling after hearing your voice and I am ready to tolerate your shouting and your taunts since I deserve this, but I need you for the rest of my life. Yes, it's fine with me. And I promise I will help you to forget this matter. I will talk sweetly with you dear. I believe my love will surely make you forget about every bad thing.'

'And I will help you to come out of the situation of Aakash Bhaiya. I will find any way so you can end the relationship with him.'

'Thank you Jaanji. I love you. I know, instead of you, if anyone else was present, then he wouldn't forgive me in this matter. I am so thankful to Godji and you. Thanks a ton for loving me so much.'

'It's fine dear.'

Two days passed since then and I talked very less with Sakshi. I was avoiding any good topics and was sticking only to formal talks since I needed time. On the other side, everyday Ishika was asking me if everything was sorted out. She always cared for me as a friend and worried to see my sad face and cheered me up. Indirectly she was helping me to forget that matter.

I replied to her, 'I will make everything normal once I go home.'

At last, the day came when I met her. On the 18 February, we met in a mall. We found one place appropriate to talk about private matters. We sat there, and I scolded her a lot. Everything was in running my mind and I was continuously yelling at her. In anger, I said, 'I don't need your resolution anymore. And I am never going to kiss you, because whenever I hear the word 'kiss', I imagine Aakash's face kissing you on your lips. I can never kiss you on your lips. I know myself; I will never be able to forget all this and will never be able to do roman with you.'

Though I was angry, on the other side, my heart was observing her. She was a sincere girl who was hearing all my talks and bowing down her head like a little child who made a mistake and the teacher scolded him. She was the best.

When my anger increased, I shouted, 'You did all this though you were in a relationship with me. It means either you are an idiot or a cheat. I know you love me, so your honesty shows that you are not a cheat. You only say that any boy would like to be with a girl who is an idiot.'

She replied politely with acute voice, 'There is one boy who will love to be with that girl and even help make her smarter, so no-one else says she is an idiot. And it's you my Malavji. It's fine if you don't need a resolution. It's ok if you will never do roman with me in our future life. I love you dearji. I knew that love is not only physical attraction and learned this from you only.'

'Sakshi...'

'Dear, I know I hurt you. I should have stopped Aakash, but I didn't apply my brains at that moment, but I promise I will take care of the next time, because you made me realise how I am, but now you are with me, so it will never happen again. I am so sorry.'

Her eyes have tears... My heart melted with her voice and her eyes.

I said to her, 'Okay, it's fine. Let's go.'

She replied, 'Where?'

I angrily said, 'Don't you trust me?'

She bowed down her eyes, 'Ok ji, sorry. Let's go.' Actually, I acted, I was not angry anymore. Whatever happened had happened; that time had already passed, so I wanted to make everything normal. I took her to the highway bridge, where many couples used to sit and enjoy. But she did not know about that place. But when she reached, she felt good; but she was still not smiling as I was acting angrily. I told her to sit down on the vehicle only. I sat on the bridge near her legs angrily.

I ordered her, 'Stop crying, I hate tears.'

She tried to hide her tears but was unable as tears were rolling down on her cheeks again and again.

I shouted, 'Better close your eyes for some time.'

Listening to my sound voice, she panicked and soon she closed her eyes.

I took an anklet from my pocket and made her wear it. She opened her eyes as I touched her and watched me making her wear it. She wiped her tears and felt too happy.

I said, 'Happy Valentine's Day Dearji.'

She felt very happy, and by seeing her happy, I too felt happy.

She replied, 'Yes Jaanji, now I am ready to say, that yes I want to be your valentine.'

I smiled and touched her cheeks.

She said, 'You were acting like you are angry.'

I said, 'You are very scared of me.'

She came down from the vehicle and sat beside me, so the public couldn't see us as we were behind the vehicle and said, 'Now your turn to close eyes dearji.'

I was expected that might be she too brought some gift for me, either for saying sorry or for Valentine's. So, I closed my eyes. She came close to me and suddenly kissed my cheeks. I opened my eyes and saw her but her eyes were closed. This was our first physical kiss on cheeks.

She said with very sweet voice, 'This feeling was not present when that bastard kissed me'.

'Jaan, I will help you to forget and you will help me to come out from the situation, as we are still one. From today after this moment, our soul has become one.' Finally we both became happy after suffering all the shocks. We spent a good time after that in good talks. She asked me, 'Dearji, I was following my part of the resolution very properly. Can't you kiss me at least on cheeks once?' I kissed her on her forehead and said, 'I still wish to do physical romance after the marriage.'

I replied, 'Yes Jaan.' At last, we ended our date. I dropped her home and went back to college. Ishika understood that everything was sorted out as she can easily read my face. Slowly again Sakshi and I talked normally. I did a little less roman, as at some weak points, I still got angry due to Aakash, but we both were helping each other. She continued following her resolution.

March passed thus and in April it was her sister's wedding in Ujjain. The marriage functions were in the Ashram but she was not attending them just because she knew that I didn't like it when she went to the ashram even though she doesn't like to see the face of Aakash. Though I was had holidays in college, I refused to go in her sister's wedding as I was just invited by Sakshi, that too unofficially. But yes, as it was a holiday, so I planned to roam around Ujjain with Ishika and Amit. Amit stayed in Ujjain itself and had our common college friend. We both went together to Ujjain, and he joined us with her girlfriend.

I went to Ujjain to get a chance to attend the wedding as at least I can see my love. Neither I get any chance, nor did I dare to do so lest my mood gets spoiled. But then I thought I brought Ishika here for sightseeing so I must make her happy. So, we four went for a movie. But it was not very good. We watched an action movie, *Tezz* starring Ajay Devgan. Ishika was telling me again and again, 'Please Malav, don't start running like Ajay Devgan. It's a movie.'

Yes, it's my bad habit, whenever I am watching a movie, I watch it so carefully that I feel I am in it. After it, we went for having an ice-cream. We had fun. It was nice meeting the love birds. Her girlfriend also had a good and friendly nature. At last, we caught the train back to Indore. I even enjoyed Ishika's company. I shared my experience of Indore with Sakshi after a few days; she even shared with me the experience of her didi's wedding.

Lastly, I just feel that I handled my relationship. We both saved our love and the important thing is we are happy. Love you Sakshi.

CHAPTER TEN

The Entry of a Villain

As soon as second-year ended, I joined a piano class to pass my time in summer vacation. Even Sakshi's college was off, so she was free, but she refused to join classes. Instead, she was learning household works from her mom. Arti was not still at home, as after college, she went to Delhi, to complete her internship in summer vacation. Priya di was happy in her married life, and Kruti ma'am was busy in her new job. I used to meet Sakshi, but only small meetings not dates as she had college holidays so she couldn't make any excuses at home and it wasn't easy for her to get out of her house. Sometimes I even complained to her about our small meetings. I used to tell that I need a full day of yours, but she always refused it by giving excuses. Anyway, I didn't force her, as she might be feeling insecure or afraid after our last date on Valentine's Day. After all, she is a girl. Once she became ready to spend one full day with me, but in June as her college would reopen then. Life was going well as usual. I love to learn new things like piano and learn a lot from yesterday's situation. I was happy that I handled such a sensitive matter pertaining to our relationship. I was feeling more mature than yesterday. One morning she called me and asked, 'Dearji, my one brother cum friend wants to meet me, so shall I give him permission?'

I asked, 'Is he your cousin?'

She replied, 'No, he became my friend in a facebook. I informed you about him once that I used to chat with him. His name is Ricky Dhanwani. Slowly our chats increased, and he treated like his sister. He is a friend of my cousin's brother in Mumbai. I met him casually.'

'You mean he is specially coming to meet you from Bombay?'

'Yes, he wants to.'

'Will he inform you about your meeting at his home or in that of your cousin brother?'

'No, if my brother came to know, he would beat me.'

'Then, Sakshi, I am so sorry. You are not allowed to meet him. He is not your boyfriend. Right?'

'If he was my boyfriend, then who are you? Don't be stupid. I told you that he is like my brother.'

I shouted a little, 'But I don't trust any of your brothers after the matter of Aashish. And I know how some boys are!'

'Okay dearji, I will say no to him, but please don't shout. You know that if you shout, automatically tears come to my eyes.'

'Okay, I will not shout.'

We ended our call. I thought about this matter. I know she treats him like a brother, but I don't trust the word 'sister' in her case. Ricky Dhanwani was six years older than us, and he is a good professor in a college. But still, he is a bachelor. Can anyone come from Bombay to here just for a meeting with a friend or a sister? He met her at facebook in January. I know everything about him. She always informed me about her matters. I shared this matter with Dipti di just casually. Dipti di knew about it, as she cared for me at Indore in the first year. So, one day, during a casual conversation, I asked her about this, and she said, 'Don't treat your girlfriend like this. If she wished to go, then let her go. Why does she need to take your permission in every matter? She is your girlfriend, not your servant. Girls have the full right to enjoy their independence.'

Dipti di was right. I can't trust him, but I can trust her. I called back and informed, 'Hey, if you want to meet, then call him, I am sorry and I want to assure you that from now onwards, you don't need to ask me for my permission regarding anything, you are my special friend, not my slave. I am not your master and you are always free to do what you feel is right.' After all, I know she wanted to meet him. If she is happy, then I am also happy. Everybody in their life should have such space. But till I called, it was late, as the plan was already cancelled by Ricky.

After a week, Arti was back to home and so was her sister, Princess. So, we all planned for the meeting. Princess' boyfriend was also going to come, so I invited Sakshi, and for the very first time, I was going to introduce Sakshi to everyone face to face. We all decided to meet on Friday. But on Thursday again Ricky called her and asked her for a meeting. She agreed this time. So, he came on Friday. So, this time Sakshi went with him, and I went with my friends. As I was insecure, I took a promise from Sakshi that she will text me in every hour wherever she will go. I was worried because I know Sakshi was too innocent and another thing, I don't know Ricky. I have never talked or met him. She went with him in the morning. And I went out with my friends after lunch. She was sending me a message every hour. First, she went to the Temple with him then she got wet with him in the rain. He was luckier than me. In the evening when we were going back around 5:30, I texted Sakshi, 'Can you join us for 5 minutes? I want to introduce you to my friends. And I think you have spent enough time with your Ricky friend/brother.'

She denied and said, 'Yes, but I have to teach my students at 6, you know. So, it's already late. I also have to drop Ricky Bhaiya to his hotel.'

I replied, 'What? Is he going to stay?'

'Yes, he came for two days. You don't know?'

'No, I did not know that before.'

'Okay, take care and now text me when you reach home. Drive carefully.'

'Yes dearji, maximum will reach home by 6:30.'

I came back home at around 6:00. I waited for her text and was reading her previous text. In reality, I was feeling very bad because she gave him almost her whole day. He was luckier than me. He got a chance to be with my Sakshi during the rain. He went to the Temple of Ambaji where I had wished to go with her. It was the same Temple; I went after Priya di's engagement. He got a chance to spend time with her in the garden. As time passed, I was feeling angry. It was almost 8:00 but still her text did not come. I was worried, so I called her, and she received it and said, 'Will call you back in half an hour.'

I asked, 'But where are you?'

She replied, 'I am still with my friend. He needs a SIM card, so I was late. I will reach home soon.'

And she disconnected the call. I was furious now. She was not ready to meet my friends for 5 minutes due to her tuitions and now she missed her entire class just for him. It means she went with him from 11:00 AM till 8:00 PM. In a one-and-a-half-year relationship, she had never spent 9 hours in a day with me. I was angry and awaited her call. I have to stop her from going with him tomorrow. Whatever I have wished for, she has fulfilled with him. She called me around 8:45 PM, and I was angry.

First, I received a call and said, 'Hello dear. Reached home?'

She was too happy. Her voice indicates how much she enjoyed it. She added, 'Yes, I reached just 15 minutes back. But as I was out of home for so much time, hence mom was scolding me. I just got a chance to call you. I want to share a lot. I enjoyed it a lot. I enjoyed his driving, and even he hugged me while going back. And you know, he got to know that I am continuously informing anyone, so he felt terrible, as he asked, 'Don't you trust me?' I had no answer. So tomorrow I am not going to text you. But then I talked sweetly with him, so he became normal soon. He is the best guy.'

By hearing her voice, I forget my anger. Though her sentences were hurting me, seeing her happy, I was double happy. I just replied to her, 'Dearji, if he is too close with you, then why don't you tell him about us? We will feel good if any one person from your side supports us. And another reason I am saying this is because I don't want to feel more insecure. And will you meet him tomorrow also from 11:00 to 8:00?'

She replied, 'I will try to share about us and no tomorrow up to 4:00. Why? Do you feel any pangs of jealousy?'

'Yes, a little (*Thodi Thodi*).'

'Don't worry, dearji, he is my brother and respects me a lot. He hugged me but as a sister. He is my brother, that's why he has guts to hug, not like you. *Fattu*![Coward]'

'When he is in a relationship, at that time he will be the same.'

'Okay, now I am too tired, so I need to sleep soon. Can I?'

'Yes sure.'

But later I saw that she was online on facebook, so I texted her, 'You said you want to sleep.'

She replied, 'Yes, but he took a new Sim card, so he wants to chat. Don't feel jealous, Jaan. He especially came for me, just two days. I am for you for the whole life.'

'Okay, dearji. Enjoy with your brother.'

The next morning, she called me before going. But I requested her a lot for sending me her updates on text. She agreed and sent two messages after which she did not send any. I called her, but she didn't receive it. I went for piano classes, but my mind was somewhere else. I thought like Aakash, if he does something, then what will she do? She even can't push him! No, not again. Many bad thoughts were coming to my mind, so I took permission from Sir for one call and called her also. This time she disconnected my call. May be that Ricky disconnected my call. It was almost three in the afternoon. Last I heard, she was in the Mall two hours ago. My hands were shivering while playing the piano due to negative thoughts.

I couldn't continue, so I decided to go. I informed Sir that I needed to go for some emergency, and went to that Mall. It was a huge mall. It was almost impossible to search for her in there but I found her sitting on the sofa in the clothes section of children's wear. She was sitting comfortably with him, and both were laughing and talking. Watching her, at least the bad thoughts went out of my mind. I hid behind the pillar, and called her again, in front of him, she disconnected my call also. I thought about going in front of her, but I thought what if he doesn't like it of what if he says that I don't trust her.

He easily had a point that if I trusted Sakshi, then I should not have gone to the mall in the first place. But my worry made me do so. Anyways, since my concern is long gone, I must not disturb her anymore because she is safe and okay. Besides this, now I know that she is enjoying it. Hence I decided not to bother her anymore. I don't have any doubt about her. I was afraid of my bad thoughts. Finally, I came out of my mall. My body was not anymore, shivering. I texted her, 'Dearji, no need to do any more messages. Enjoy.'

She thought I messaged her in anger, so within 5 minutes, she called back. I was on the way back home. I stopped and received her call. She said, 'He doesn't like if I am using a cell phone again and again. Please dearji, don't worry, I am fine.'

I replied, 'Dearji, I had not texted you in anger. I sat peacefully and thought if I was at his place, even if I felt bad. Hence I told not to message so you both can enjoy.'

Sakshi, 'Thank you for understanding.'

I reached home and started my computer, and I opened Sakshi's account on facebook, and read the chat between her and Ricky.

In every message, he addressed her as 'sis', and similarly she addressed him as 'bro'. I read the chat in detail. They spent very good time with each other. Sakshi had informed me only topics, but they had discussed their whole life yesterday. By reading her chat, I understood that they both are very attached to each other. I thought he was the right person for supporting us from her side. So, I decided before he went back, Sakshi must tell him everything about us, so if he wants to meet me, then he can. But now I can't call, I can't disturb him again, I have to wait for her call. It was five already. Soon she will call since she decided to come back by 4. She called me at 8 o'clock, I received it and asked her, 'Have you informed him about us?'

'No.'

'Why are you late today also?'

'He specially came for me from Bombay. How can I tell him that I want to go back?'

'Okay, No problem. Dearji, I read your chat. So, I think you must inform him about us before he goes. He seems attached to you, so maybe if he comes to know later, he will get hurt, and if you tell him now, maybe I can meet him if he wants.'

'Ya, you are right. Let me call him.'

'Jaan Jaan, wait.'

'Yes, dearji.'

'Promise me. There will be no effect of this on our relationship.'

'Obviously Jaan. Love you always.'

'Okay. Go and tell him about us.'

This decision changed my life. When she informed him, he became too sentimental and started to cry. He felt terrible as she had hidden about us for a very long time. So, he told her that she broke his trust. Sakshi called me and said, 'Dearji, I need some days to handle him as I hurt him.'

I replied to her, 'Okay, No problem. Just remember there will be no change in our relationship. And do whatever possible by you but make him calm, as he got hurt by us, not only by you.'

The next day, I called Sakshi and asked his status. She informed, 'He is driving his bike, exceeding the speed limit and without a helmet. He is continuously crying. He has not even eaten anything since morning.'

'Oh my god, but how did he get hurt to such an extent?'

'Dearji, he took a promise from me that I will not hide anything from him on promise day. So now he thinks I broke his trust. He already asked about it many times, but I always replied to him negatively.'

'Okay, shall I talk to him?'

'No, he will be angrier. Give me some more time.'

'Sure Jaan.'

After ending our call, I feel weird. I thought now he might be crossing his limits. How can she inform him about us on promise day? It was 9 February and at that time he was new to her. I was on her first priority. Anyway maybe in his sentimental mood, he is unable to understand her.

As days passed, instead of peace, the situation was becoming worse. He calmed down, but he requested Sakshi, 'Dear Sakshi, you broke my trust. If you want me back as your brother, then you have to stop this relationship at least for a year. If your feelings are true, they will remain forever. I am just asking a year for your studies.'

Sakshi informed me about this, but I replied to her, 'Dearji, I am delighted with him. Yes, feelings remain forever as we love each other truly, but I don't trust time. Please make him understand that we have a habit of each other.'

She agreed. Some days passed and I realised that my love Sakshi is avoiding me now.

The worst feeling is when we know the person is doing wrong, but neither we are able to stop them from doing so nor we are able to handle their wrong doings. I don't want her to ignore me, but even I am not letting her stop doing so. Maybe my heart wants to know if she can live without me. As days were passing, I was feeling very bad. That villain entered Sakshi's life after me, but he is making her dance on his fingers. She even stopped following her resolution. Slowly she was skipping talking for a day or two and later only once in a week. I was unable to tolerate more, so I called her and forced her to meet me. Initially, she was not ready, but later I did some emotional melodrama, at least on my birthday, one last time. Hence, she got ready. Ricky met her once and made my life worse. I am waiting for my birthday, though I can predict it will be worst day and it totally depends on Sakshi.

\#

After five days, my college reopened and third year started. My feelings worsened. We both were so attached that we shared every small or large matter. So, I was feeling her absence. Hence, I was sure she will also feel the same. But I know, girls are too obstinate and too strong for their decision. So, she will not change her decision at any cost. But then too, I decided to call once more. I again called her after a week and tried to convince her a lot but she was not ready to hear a word too. I tried to make her realise about our feelings of true love, moonlight walks, told her every sweet moment of our life but in the end she replied angrily, 'Don't you understand, at present I don't have any feelings for anyone.' And she disconnected my call. Her words made me feel dead inside. Now it was really ending. How can she say such words? Feelings are not things that they go back and forth.

Everybody knew that I loved her more than I loved myself. Due to the break of such an excellent relationship, I was a mess. I was unable to concentrate on my studies. Along with studies, I am not able to maintain my other relations, like I started to take out my frustrations on my parents and friends. My grades dropped too, and I was fighting almost with every friend, including Ishika. I had noticed myself and my friends. They used to refer to me as an 'angry young man'. My comedy was turned into silence, smile to madness. I was crossing my every limit. I stopped talking to my many casual friends. Once there was a time, at any cost, I was always smiling, as I have my power with me. i.e. Sakshi. But now the same girl has become my weakness.

Each second passing makes me feel sadder and realize her absence. I badly need her. I need a friend. I called Arti and informed her everything. She said, 'Malav if she went, it doesn't mean that life is stopped. We have to move on with time.'

Arti knew that I would not listen to a word against Sakshi, though she was angry at Sakshi, calmly she said, 'Why are you not becoming a true lover who can do anything for their partner? She just needs a year from you Malav, then she will be back, then why are you going into depression? Why are you so sentimental? Why are you fighting with everyone?'

I replied with tears in my eyes but a little louder voice, 'One year. Arti do you think it's only tough for me? No, it's impossible for me now. Yes, it may be possible for her since this was her decision, not ours. If at present, she doesn't have any feelings then what miracle will happen in a year?'

Arti, 'But might be she has some reason behind it. Please Malav, stop crying like a baby and respect her decision. You know she loves you truly, then whatever you are feeling, same she will feel. So, think like this if she came to know that her distance had broken you fully, she would feel guilty from inside. Do you want to make your love guilty?'

I wiped my tears and replied to her, 'She will not feel bad about anything at present, since she doesn't have feelings for anyone including me. Whatever is my condition she will not be affected. And if she has some reason behind it, then also she must share that with me, as she knows that without sharing, we are both unhappy. So better be unhappy after sharing at least we feel support for each other. You know Arti, she told me that after a year she wants me to be the same Malav, like I am at least school other in starting college. But after a year, it will be the future, she is not ready to understand that we have to live in the present, neither in the past nor in the future. I am dying each and every moment without her. I blame myself that I failed to make her realise that we are not two. I failed to make her understand that at present, I needed her the most. I might be unable to understand her, as her decision is right according to her way of thinking, but not mine. I might fail in my love dear.' She too got tears in her eyes. I heard her voice while crying. So, I added, 'I made you also cry. Sorry.'

Arti replied, 'Malav, these tears are for those friend who is pure-hearted understanding people, but at present he is in deep depression. Hence he is not ready to come out from it still he did not get his special friend back. So please relax, and take your time to come back from your depression. I will wait for you.'

I replied, 'Okay Arti, but promise me. You will not tell about my situation to Priya di. She is busy in her married life. Please, it's a request.'

'Okay Promise.' Arti ended the call.

Next day, Ishika asked, 'Hey, Did you have a fight with Bhumi?'

I replied affirmatively.

She responded, 'That's why you are not behaving properly. Anyways, take your time, but I must suggest, keep your personal life away from friends.'

I thanked her. I called Kruti ma'am, but she was in Delhi for some reason.

#

Some days passed in depression. Then came a long weekend where everybody went home, but I decided to stay there only. Ishika called me in the evening, but I didn't receive her call as I knew she will also go home and will ask about my status, but I don't want to say anything to her. She is already worried for me and in this matter I don't want anyone as Arti was unable to help me. Hence I know no-one can help me in this matter. I started my laptop and watched a movie - *Devdas*.

Though I had already watched this movie in the theatre and slept as I didn't like it at all. I don't know why I decided to watch that movie; maybe I am already feeling the absence of my Paro. I realised one fact of human nature that **when a person is suffering from his wrong time, indeed he will find the way for becoming weaker**. After completing my movie, I made my bed to sleep and locked the door, switched the light off and took my cell phone and I decided to call Sakshi once again. This would surely be my last talk. I called her and said, 'Sakshi, just think from my perspective once, put yourself in my place and try to feel what I am feeling! I was doing the same from the last few months. I placed myself at your place, so I still respect your decision, but now it's more than a month. Dearji, can't you just try this for me once? I want you to be with me at any cost.'

She shouted so loudly, 'Why should I follow your advice? You are nothing to me at present. If you truly love me, then wait for me for one year. If Godji wishes, we will surely be one in future.'

She never talked to me so angrily, so even I got anger in me and replied to her, 'I know what Godji wishes. If he had not wished, then we have never met, and never became too close. I just want to know what you wish. So last time I am asking, reply to me after thinking twice. Don't you need me? Do you love me?'

On the spot, she replied, 'I don't have any feelings for you, and it's my final answer.' She disconnected my call.

Tears welled up in my eyes, my heart... I cried a lot after it. My bed sheet and my pillow become wet. Feelings are not toys and are not made for playing and are neither for a short period. Once they come, it remains forever in the heart's corner. I don't remember exactly when I slept, but lastly, I watched my cell phone till 02:07 AM, 20 July. And when I woke up, I was shocked after watching time. It was 02:07 PM, 20 July. Maybe I had not slept properly for the last few days, hence today morning I didn't wake up. Soon I realised my eyes are still wet. My head was feeling heavy. I kept my room open and went outside in the hottest afternoon from my society.

I turned the right-hand side of my society, where there was a bus stand. I sat there alone. Sakshi's words are still echoes in my ears. Suddenly one voice came from the right-hand side of my head and said to me, 'Hey Malav, committing suicide in the nearest canal of your college is better than living such a bad life. Due to the present style of your living life, everyone is unhappy: Your Friends, Your Family, Your Sakshi. So, it's better to end your life friend.' I turned my face on the right side. There was a boy looking like me only, but his skin was bright red in colour.

Only there was a ring at some gap in his head. It was no one else than my own soul. I was shocked by seeing him. Still today I thought it only occurs in Bollywood movies, but in reality it was happening. Even once Ishika told me that she believes that a red and orange soul for every person exists. I replied to him, 'Are you crazy? **Love is not the only relation in life**. I have many other relations in my life. My parents will cry more than I am crying at present if I will suicide. So, at any cost, I can't end my life, I may be a loser, but I am not coward who ran away from his life and accepted death. I just completed two years of my college. Still, I have to face many more phases of my life.'

He replied to me, 'Do you think that your parents are happy to see you like this?' Suddenly a second voice came from my left side and said, 'No, Malav. Your Sakshi wants to see you happy.' I moved my face on the left-hand side and watched him. He was also the same looking like him, but his skin was bright blue in colour. He was my second soul. I was expecting the orange one according to what Ishika had told me. Maybe Ishika told blue and orange, then from where did red come? Anyways stop thinking about colours, let's focus on the situation.

He added, 'Malav, please don't commit suicide. Your Sakshi will not be happy to see your dead body.'

I angrily replied to him, 'Don't bring her name up. She will not be affected to see my dead body because she doesn't have any feelings for me. She wants me in the future, but I need her at present. Can you bring her from nowhere? Suppose I end my life now, and then what will she do? At present, due to her absence and her words, I am feeling too bad, and that's the reason you both are present. So please don't dare say her name.'

By hearing this second blue soul vanished. I respect my parents a lot, so I shouted on my red soul also and told him to go and added – 'I will not commit suicide at any cost. It's a crime. So just get out from here.' So my red soul also vanished. Yes, they both were a part of my imagination.

Then in anger, I stood up from the bus stand and suddenly what happened to me, I also don't know, but I noticed that time was running slowly, only I can run fast. I saw a cute little girl in front of me on the crossroads. She was crying and confused in traffic. Someone was shouting on the opposite side. I saw there was a woman in a sari, and she was screaming, 'Sakshi, be careful. Please somebody save my daughter.'

And then I turned my face towards the little girl who was crying and shouting, 'Mummy, where are you?' and then I noticed one truck coming towards baby Sakshi. As soon as I heard the name of a little girl, my mind and heart told me that I couldn't commit suicide, but I can save her because her life is more important to me. She is a child. The very next moment I jumped on the road and pushed baby Sakshi towards her mother and at the same time the truck smashed my head, and I flew in air and fell at 5 feet far from that position where my head had been obstructed by the divider. It was like a movie scene where everything was happening for me, but for others, this happened within a moment.

Everyone gathered around me, bleeding started, and the road was full of blood from my brain. Slowly I become unconscious and closed my eyes, but my lips are just saying the words, 'Sakshi...Sakshi...' Suddenly I felt a vibration in my whole body, especially near my head. But I was unable to open my eyes. Then I was able to hear a song, *'Tumhi ho bandhu... Sakha tumhi... Tumhi din Chadhey... Tum hi din dhale...'* [A song from movie Cocktail]. My ears forced my eyes to open. I was feeling a headache. I kept my left hand on my head and tried to see here and there that from who is singing a song when I am in such condition. On my right side, I saw a girl sitting beside me. I expected Sakshi, but sooner I realized it was not Sakshi, it was Ishika.

I closed my eyes, cleaned it and saw again it was not Sakshi. I did the same for 3 to 4 times, but the same result. Finally, I realised it was my cell-phone which was showing me Ishika's face as I kept it as a contact photo and the vibration and the song were also a result of her calls. I saw the time in my cell phone. It was

07:02 AM, 20 July only. I saw myself in the mirror, just a dot on my head.

I shouted to myself, 'Oh my God, it was such a scary and a melodramatic dream.' I almost died. My head might get hurt due to obstruction of the wall in sleep. I felt my face. It was still wet and again I went into the same thinking as last night that Sakshi had no feelings for me. But I felt the phone ringing. So, I picked up the call and said with a very low voice, 'Hello.'

Ishika, 'If you had not received my call this time, I might have come to your room.'

Malav, 'Ishika, you have not gone to your home. Why?'

She replied, 'I am outside your building. Come downstairs and then we'll talk.'

I was shocked; she reached till my room. I washed my face and went down.

I said, 'Good Morning.'

She replied, 'Is your morning good? Just look at yourself Malav.'

'Ishika, I had a very bad dream. I hope my dream comes true, as I know morning dreams always come true.'

'See what you are talking about. Though the dream was bad, you want God fulfil it.'

'Ishika!'

'Shut up, Malav. I didn't go home just for you. You didn't receive my call from yesterday. The whole night I am worrying for you because I know you. You love her truly. I told you to keep your personal life far from friends, but I didn't say keep your friends far from you and your personal life. I am always there for you, my friend. I love to be your listener. Malav, by sharing, you will feel better, your heart might suffer less. Please.'

'Ishika, thanks a lot for caring. Okay, we will meet after I get fresh up.'

'Okay, I am waiting.'

I came back to the room and took a bath, and then I planned to meet her. We went for a walk as usual, where I shared my whole story.

She just replied one sentence, which helped me a lot, 'Malav, I don't know much about love, but I heard that *love is a feeling, if it's your love than it's only yours, it doesn't depend what other person wants, it actually doesn't matter.* So I suggest that *you don't think what she asked for, just do what you feel.*'

She was the best. Unbelievable! Ishika always answered me, many times without knowing the actual question.

She added, 'Don't force her for anything. Let her do what she wants. As far as I know you, you just love her in your way. If she wants patience and your heart want to respect her decision, and then show her that. I know you can do it. Move on Friend. The world is too good.'

Finally, I enjoyed the mini-vacation with her. Many times, I felt weak, but she supported me as my best friend. Lastly, I decided that I will wait for her. She has kept her condition. But I have feelings, and I will wait for her. And the moments which make me feel weak; I will try to eliminate them. Sakshi was right that I should start to live like I was in school. So, I will try my best not to miss her as that makes me weak, and then disaster situations can occur. I have many friends in college. I will move on and will see where my life takes me. Thanks, a lot, to Ishika.

And Sakshi, I Love You a lot. I am waiting for you. Come Soon.♥

CHAPTER ELEVEN

The Result of Waiting for True Love

My college friends helped me in that year to let life live without her in my daily routine, but everyone knows that deep inside I was waiting for her. I was sure that my decision to wait for my love is right. It's absolutely okay. In the course of true love you have to take certain exams and I am going to clear this exam for sure; I am positive. Time is tough; every night, I just text her, "Miss you. Good night" on an email created by me on her name, just a way to make fool to my heart that she is with me in my imagination. I gave a grand party to my roommates on her birthday. Many times, my friends used to call me '*Aashiq*'. Since I was a huge Bollywood buff, I was happy to hear that word.

Many friends advised me to be practical. They told me it was impossible that after a year's gap, the same situation and same bonding will be there. I used to reply to them as well as to myself that the feeling of true love never changes and we can't lose this to anyone, or anything till we accept to lose. I am not going to lose, since my feeling towards my love is very true and I am going to wait for her. The only person who supports my decision against her own will is Ishika, since she knew everything about the past of my Sakshi. Sometimes I feel how girls really understand deep pain like Ishika, so I concluded how much Sakshi is suffering that she also knew that she is the cause of pain still she is giving. *Kuch to majburi hogi* [There must be some reason behind this].

The only fact here is that it literally affected my studies. My heart was not ready to take any interest in any work or studies, but sometimes I used to push it and involve my friends to keep all my sorrows aside, but that was temporary. When I became weak, I used to say to myself, 'Come on Malav, it's just a year, then she will be mine and I will be hers.'

I really don't know how this year passed and the date of external exams came. I don't care about studies; I was just waiting for my exams to be over so that I can go to my Sakshi. Not a single exam of mine went well but still I was happy on my last day of my exam. Everyone went back home for vacation, so everyone was happy, but only I was had a different reason. We waved each other good bye and I knew I was alone in this city and was walking towards my room. I had mixed feelings now that one year was finally over. I wondered about the status of my relationship. As soon as I reached the gate of the society where my PG was, Ishika jumped behind the wall and said,

'Surprise!' I asked, 'Why are you here?'

She replied, I felt that my friend needs me, so I delayed my plan to go home.

'Oh dear, you are too good, you can read anything, I hugged her.'

'If I am so good, kindly tell me the real name of Bhumi, please?'

'Sakshi'.

'Wow! Nice Name!'

'Thanks.'

She asked, 'So what's the plan?'

I replied, 'I even don't know. But from my common friends I came to know that her exam as well as her convocation is over. But, I am unable to understand how to initiate the conversation after a year. I don't know about her feelings. Will she have feelings? Will she be excited like me? Ishika, I think I should call her directly to avoid any kind of misunderstanding, but what if she disconnects my call and blocks me forever? What will I do then? What if her phone is with her dad or that villain? I don't want to take any risk. But I can't just sit and relax without hearing her voice once. I need to do something.'

'Malav, relax, we will find a way.'

'And what's that?'

'I don't know, let's think.'

'I got an idea, I can't call, but I can call from an unknown number, Ishika can you give me your phone to call?'

Clearly her face showed she didn't wish to give her phone to me but she was here just to help me so she can't deny. But she was fortunate since her mobile phone slipped from my hand and it broke. I apologised and I told her to let me repair her mobile. So, I gave her my mobile and told her to go back to your room, I will come soon. She agreed. I gave her mobile for repair where they told me that only the glass had broken along with the power off button, so it would be ready again in another half hour. I found a PCO nearby only, so I went and dialled Sakshi's number after a year.

She picked up a call and said, 'Hello!' in her beautiful voice and sweet accent. I was falling for her again just with her voice. She repeated 4 to 5 times, hello, then I realised I had come back to the real world, and in quick response I just said her name, 'Sakshi' She recognised my voice and disconnected the call. I called thrice again but she didn't pick up. The next day, I tried to call her from my phone at noon but she didn't pick up and then again in the evening.

So, for the next two days, around 20 calls have been placed to her from my side. Now, I feel she might have blocked me. On the sixth day, Ishika and I went for having evening snacks, I asked for suggestions from her.

She said, 'I don't know, you better know about your love story'

I asked, 'Why am I feeling that you are not supporting me on this?'

She replied, 'Hey friend, I supported you whole year with my whole heart, you know that many times I went opposite to my mom, just to support you like this time. It's just I don't have any idea for such situations, that's why I am reacting like this, else I am always with you, I will support you in your every decision dear.'

I felt good to hear such words, that she will support me in any decision. I was waiting and thinking for any new idea to click to my mind or heart. I can understand that after such a gap, it takes time to bond again. This fear of girls can be natural. I have waited so long, I know she also waited long, though she must have an unknown fear. I believe time will find a way to start our relationship again. On that night, I was on terrace just to get some fresh air, my phone rang, it was Sakshi! Yes finally it was her. I have a wide smile on my lips and tears in my eyes upon seeing her name on my screen. I received her call.

She said, 'Hello.'

I replied, 'Hi Sakshi'

'How are you?'

With a small pause to pour my tears, I replied, 'I am fine, Thank you. What about you?'

'I am also good, I want to inform you something, but please stop crying.'

'I am okay. Let me pour my tears properly out, and yes whatever you want to inform me, inform me later, first guess where I am?'

'Where ? Don't say below my home!'

'No Jaan, I am at that place, where we started our first imagination in the moon light.'

I expected her to say "Aww" but instead she cried and disconnected the call by saying, 'Good bye Malav.'

I was shocked and confused.

Hey Diary, just listen to my thoughts.

She called herself. Does it mean she misses me? But then why did she say goodbye? She said that she wanted to inform me, but I feel now I was the one who in overexcitement made her miss our memories. *Itne time baad baat ki thi, thoda slow jana chahiye tha yaar!* [We had word after a year or more, I guess I should have moved on slowly]

Anyway now, I couldn't do anything except being positive. Have patience Malav, there will surely be a way to start back again our never-ending relationship to get our fruitful result of waiting.

Next morning, I asked Ishika to do me a favour, to call her at home and talk like a friend, receptionist, or any way for an interview or something. She refused to do so and added, 'If she doesn't want to talk, then no matter how many times you call, she won't do it and you can't force a girl, Malav.'

I was disappointed to hear this and I was going back to my fears, Ishika held my hand and said, 'No, Malav, you are not going back to that state, we will find a solution.'

I informed her about yesterday's call and tried to convince her by saying, 'See, she called on her own will, it clearly indicates she also wants to talk. But there must be something which is stopping her from talking to me, may be the obstacle is the gap of a year, or moment she called, I want to remove that obstacle, I want to help her in that, but that is possible only after meeting her, that's why Ishika, I request you, please help me to let her meet me once.' She agreed.

She called at landline number of her home, 'Hello,'

Someone from her side, 'Hello'

Ishika, 'Hello, Can I talk to Sakshi? I am her friend Pooja.' She assumed Pooja is a common name in every friend list.

Someone replied, 'I am sorry Pooja, but she is in the parlour right now as you might know that day after tomorrow is a family function(disturbance of background noise),.. ceremony, so she is busy at work.'

Ishika, 'Oh yes for that reason only, actually I just need the location and timing for it. She has invited me but in a hurry she forgot to send me the details about the venue.'

Someone, 'Oh is it? Kindly note that the venue is Hotel Meghraj and timing is 7:30 PM.'

Ishika, 'Thank you.' And she disconnected the call.

I asked her about the conversation, but she was pulling my leg. But later, when I bought her two chocolates, finally she said, 'Malav, I was unable to set a date for you, but there is some family function at hotel Meghraj at 7:30 PM, may be the *opening ceremony* of some parlour or something. I couldn't get the exact details due to background noise of kids from her side, but venue and timing is surely right.'

I replied, 'Thank you so much for this help also. I know what I have to do now.'

She replied, 'Your big smile shows that you have some filmy Bollywood plans. I really don't believe in Bollywood, hence I am warning you, whatever you do, do cautiously.'

I replied, 'I don't have an exact plan, but I will work on it, actually we will work on it. You promised that you will support me and help me, right?'

'What I just did is called help, if I am not wrong.'

'How can girls sarcastic at any moment, too smart.'

'Don't be angry. Tell me how I can help you.'

'I will inform and discuss everything with you. After all you are a girl too, so you can say or help me out by letting me know what girls like. For now just pack your bag, take 2 or 3 days' clothes, we are moving to my home in another half an hour.'

'What? Are you kidding? I need to ask my mom.'

I put fingers in my ears and added, 'I am not listening, I know you will manage everything, I am going to pick you up in next 30 minutes. Bye.'

She couldn't refuse after seeing my excitement of the waiting period being over. I booked a bus, it was an overnight journey to my hometown and I already told Ishika we are not going to sleep, we have to plan a lot. We boarded the bus, and I started dictating my plan. I made a list

1) what I am going to do

2) How

3) Where

4) When.

Around 3 am, I saw that Ishika was sleepy so I asked her to sleep. She slept in a minute, but I was very happy with my imagination. I planned everything that I will do on the next day and after the day. The very first work, I will inform my family that I have love in my life and we have passed the test of patience. Soon we shall be engaged and after I am settled, I am going to marry Sakshi.

I laughed on myself and said, 'Malav, stop yourself, you are moving ahead too fast!' I didn't realise but three hours passed and at 6 AM we reached. I woke up Ishika, she was in deep sleep, she asked, 'How far your home is from station?'

I replied, 'We are not going home, I came here for Sakshi. If I will go home, my mom will hug me till noon then who will do the work for my best day.'

She replied, 'I really don't know from where you have so much energy, anyways where we are heading then?'

'I already have bookings for us in a safe hotel.'

'I trust you Malav.'

As soon as we reached, she slept and I went outside. I started with the venue and requested the owner for tomorrow's booking, but he refused as it was already booked. I informed them, 'Yes I know it has been booked, but I request you to give me some small space, and I will finish my work before their function starts, I promise.'

Finally, the owner convinced and gave me booking but the space they gave me was a terrace. I took this as a positive sign. I visited the terrace at 5:30 PM for some fresh air. On the next day, it belonged to me on the same time so I planned how to decorate it in my mind and note down on my sticky notes what materials I need for decoration. So, after venue, I booked the decorator, and bought balloons, flowers, and bouquets. I booked a musician and selected some romantic photographs for the venue. After that, I went to a cybercafé, where I made a collage of her pictures from childhood to college. I took print out of each and every picture by myself. Then I got one new idea, that I should make a PPT for childhood to adulthood photos, so I bought a projector on half day rent. Then I went to my friend's home, took a laptop which helps me to show the projector, and reached back to the room. It was already 4 PM. Ishika just completed her lunch. She asked, 'I have called you twice since morning. You don't have such decency to reply or to call your friend back who just came for you from another city.'

'Hey Ish, I know what you are doing for me is out of boundaries, but I also know that friends do that.

Anyway I ignore your questions, just listen to my plan and do me two favours.'

'How bluntly you are saying that you ignored my questions and at the same moment you are asking me for more favours. What type of a guy are you?'

'Hey, stop acting like a girl and listen to me carefully.'

She smiled and asked me to continue.

'Firstly, you have to make a playlist of instrumental romantic songs.'

She interrupted, 'Wait Malav, did you eat something? Look at your eyes idiot.'

I replied, 'Yes, see my eyes, but also see my excitement, my love towards my Sakshi, Ishika I am going to see her meet her after a year, I am going to die for her.'

She angrily shouted, 'You are going to die for sure, if you didn't obey me, eat the sandwich kept on table right now and sleep for some time, else I am going back.'

With puppy face, I moved towards the sandwich and had to obey her instructions, since I needed her. After eating, I slept for three hours. After waking up, Ishika helped me to make video collage for Sakshi and her family pictures.

Ishika asked, 'What is the second favour that you want from me?'

I replied, 'I don't know how, but you have to bring Sakshi up to the terrace since you are Pooja for her family members.'

She agreed and added, 'See, I will manage to do that. But after that I will move back to Indore, so help me with the bookings.'

I denied, 'No, you are in my city. After this event, I will introduce you to my family. I am able to do this only due to your help.'

'See Malav, I genuinely consider you as my good friend, so it's my duty to help you. I feel, timing is incorrect for my introduction into your family. First inform your family about Sakshi. I promise, I will come next time.'

'Ok dear.' I made a booking for her seat on the bus at 7 PM tomorrow so she reached her cousin's home which is just 4 hours away.

We had dinner, then she went to sleep, I went for a walk in fresh air. I didn't realise when I reached my favourite place – the bus stand and slept there only. It might be awkward for many people but this year I slept many times at the bus station itself. Since it really helps me forget my loneliness. In the morning, I woke up to the loud noise of the horn of the bus, I came back to the hotel, it was around 10:30 AM and Ishika was already ready. She instructed me to get ready soon and she ordered breakfast for me. I asked her to visit the venue for a cross check once but she suggested that we go shopping instead. 'What are you going to wear? You don't have anything special for such a big day!' I was planning to buy jeans and a t-shirt but Ishika convinced me that I looked better in formals and first time I bought one pair of clothes without the help of any family member. Later we went to Archies and bought a lot of gifts for my Sakshi.

To see such gifts, Ishika said, 'You are rich enough.'

I replied, 'No, it's not like that, but yes I am rich enough for my love.'

'Meaning?'

'Actually, I saved money by cancelling my noon tiffin for a month.'

'Are you out of your mind?'

'No, no Ishika, don't worry, I have very little appetite! Besides, my mother has given a lot of snacks for me and my roommates.'

'The real reason is that you are crazy for her.'

'For my Love!'

'No, only for her, I hope it's true love. I will pray for you.'

'It will definitely be true love, else I would not have been excited like this and God has never indicated to me that she also wants to talk.'

At 4 PM, we reached the venue and started waiting for her. At 4:30 PM the terrace was ready with balloons, even the musician was ready, and the projector was ready. I verified everything twice. I know Sindhi people are always late in functions. It was already 6 PM. After a lot of waiting, I guess the last hour was not less than a year itself. Finally, I saw a car coming.

And finally from the terrace, I got a small glimpse of my Sakshi. This time she was looking gorgeous, she was wearing a western golden kurta type one piece. She was looking stunning and very beautiful. She was wearing contact lenses in her eyes instead of spectacles. And along with that she was wearing matching earrings and bangles to make her the perfect bride for an evening. I knew she loved to get ready like every other girl.

Ishika walked towards me and handed me the tissue, 'That one in golden na? And don't make such a romantic atmosphere too emotional. I am going to send her upstairs; be ready and yes after it I will go to catch my bus. It's already 6:15PM.'

I hugged her and thanked her. She said, 'Bye and All the best.'

I don't know how, but Ishika somehow managed to bring Sakshi upstairs, as soon as both reached upstairs, Ishika sent Sakshi inside and closed the door from outside and waved a goodbye to me. On the other side, Sakshi entered from the gate and a flower shower started over her. She smiled. I feel I saw her smile after a decade.

Then I nodded to a waiter from the back side of door who went in front of Sakshi, and showed her the way, 'Ma'am, this way please.'

On the right-hand side of entrance, I had made one cave of cloth and artificial stones without light. Initially she was afraid of dark, but then the waiter instructed her, 'Ma'am, as soon as you will enter inside, the light will be on from the sensor place below the floor by your feet placed over the entrance of cave.'

She went inside and decorative lights came on and the cave was full of photos in the order from her childhood to adulthood, i.e. every birthday. Along with every photo, I had written one special thought for her. She followed the sequence of photos, which led her to another cave which includes a projector. I switched it on, which included videos of her dance and poems from her school days when she had performed on many stage shows. It also includes one drama which she performed in her family. She was really enjoying her memories. I was so excited when she saw me, what would happen? Will the same smile exist? Will she remember our whole memories and cry? Will she come and hug me tight? I am feeling nervous about what will happen. I don't want to come in front of her, since I need to see this smile forever like this only. Please God, press the pause button of her life over here only. Last but not the least, as soon as the projector shows the end, curtains came in front of the projector which has printed 'I really love you Sakshi' on it. Her smile was unbelievable, she was blushing, her heart was very happy, her face was glowing and I felt this is the time for my entry. I did not have any ring, but I do have many mixed feelings in my heart. I came in front of her by opening the curtain and she was literally shocked to see me.

Her reaction was already expected by me, but I thought it would follow a smile and hug, instead what came out of her was tears in her eyes. She was too emotional yaar. She turned around and saw the terrace again and asked, 'You did all this?' I smiled and slowly I moved towards her. She was going back and more tears were falling from her eyes. I bent down on my knees kind of in a proposed position, I said, 'I don't have a golden ring, but here I have a small ring made of your favourite thing i.e. conch (*Shankh*). Dearji, I know it's very long time since we have kept our patience, there might be mixed feelings inside you. But here ***I am to support you, to support us, to support our love, to let the world know that we cleared our exams and the most important to let you know that no matter what happens, I will be always in front of you, bowing down like at present moment so that you realise that there is a person who is going to be there only for you, always.***'

She cried upon hearing my words and turned back and was going far from me, but I held her hand and said, 'Sorry, I can't stop myself anymore.'

And I pulled her, after a year I wrapped her inside my arms, hugged her to get peace, to let her feel secure and to love her. This was the moment which I had been waiting for.

I hugged her passionately but this time it really pinched me hard inside my heart, such that the very next moment, tears rolled down from my eyes. I don't know what the reason was; it was the first time my sixth sense was telling me something is wrong. As soon as I hugged her, I realised she was not the same. Yes she was present inside my arms, but her soul was not there. At the same moment, I saw Ishika open the gate with tears in her eyes. I knew she was not going to come back as she was scheduled for her travel back to her cousin's home, but to see her it was clear that something is wrong.

But I didn't want to leave Sakshi, I want her to have same feelings which she was having with me in our good times, so I hugged her more tightly hoping she remember our bond. I put my face on her shoulder, and closed my eyes so that I can ignore what Ishika was trying to say me. I wanted this moment so badly, on one side, it was very hurtful, but on another side, I had been waiting for this hug so long. As soon as I closed my eyes, many things were going on in my imagination. In my mind, I paused everything and try to reverse the time from the present moment to the last year at a slow rate so that I could spend maximum time in our hug. I tried to remember, few hours ago, my expectations, my planning, then about yesterday night, day before it how Ishika managed this meeting by talking to Sakshi's relative, by finding the venue and time of opening *ceremony*, and the day before it, Sakshi called me and said, want to inform you something! My mind interrupted me and suddenly my eyes opened. Yes, it clicked and my heart felt very sad.

I loosened my hands. I was just going to let her free from my hug. It was really a very painful moment to describe in words, till I gathered courage and moved my lips towards her right ear and whispered, 'I really loved you till the moment I hugged you. Anyway, many congratulations for your new life and new love.' I left the hug and started walking towards the gate. Sakshi called my name, 'Malav'.

I have wanted to hear that in her voice for a year, that name from her lovely tone, but now it was not time to hear her voice. All dreams were shattered already. Ishika came forward and said, 'Sorry, I misinterpreted.' I kept fingers on her mouth and said, 'It's not your fault, God has indicated this to me several times, like your phone was broken when we were calling her call to inform, I might not understood the God's way, but I got it that it was not an opening ceremony, it was ring ceremony of my love with someone else.'

I added, 'I saw Sakshi's best smile just a few minutes ago while she was watching all this, the flowers and her childhood pictures. But that smile doesn't belong to me anymore; she assumed it was her new love that had planned this for her. How foolish I am, Ishika. Many friends in college told me to be practical. Sakshi really moved on without letting me (her true love or not) know. I ignored many friends who were trying to show me the practical situations just for this girl. Really, Ishika?' To see me like this, Ishika also becomes emotional, till she gathered courage for her friend (me) and held my hand and we moved from that place.

I asked Ishika to let me stay alone for some time. Initially she was not ready. I gave her the promise of our friendship, and finally she boarded her bus and I went to my favourite spot, i.e. the bus stop. I waited there till the sky became completely dark and there were very less people near me. On the other side, Sakshi was getting engaged with some other guy. At night, I finally cried like a baby, and moved my face towards the sky and shouted to myself or to God, 'Why? Today, I understood when people feel bad, why they blame you God, because you are the creator of unexpected situations. As a normal human being, I know everyone wants their first love to be their last love, then why do you make situations which make the people think that their love doesn't last forever. God, you can see me crying, you have seen her tears a few hours ago. We both are your children then why did you let this happen?'

Diary, I feel this is the first time that I am feeling the pain of an injection in my heart. It feels awful to have my heart pinched thus. I feel confused. I feel weak and I feel like a loser. I didn't lose from anyone else but from myself. Am I depressed? If yes, then how will I come out of it since the love of my life is never going to come back to me. She has moved on with her new partner and left me with a lot of unanswered questions which are very heavy for my heart.

Today, I am feeling anxious but I am unsure if is this anxiety or just sadness and feelings of a breakup which technically happened a long time ago but I realised it today. So, I was a fool. Please God, save me from all these bad feelings and don't let anyone of my close ones pity me. I don't want that. But God, will you care about what I really want? I don't want to write further... These tears and this pain in my heart is my gift from you. Thank you God. You made me realise that true love does not always win and wait doesn't always give fruitful results. At present, Aashish and that Aakash don't matter. Because sacrifice doesn't matter here. The only feeling I have here is of losing my self-respect. It was love or craziness for a person. No, I can't say anything bad to Sakshi, because when she was with me, she loved me the way no one ever did. Then what is wrong with me? Was this the result of my karma of previous life? I lived my whole life according to you God, be it the entry of the first girl (Arti) in my life, the possessiveness of friends, the true love story shown to me in the form of Priya di, the entry of Sakshi, her shocks on Valentine's Day. Her brother who told her to wait, and lastly I get these feelings today as a result: Stress, Depression, Anxiety, I don't feel to die or something. Actually, I don't feel anything at present. Am I made of stone? Loser stone? Aimless? Tears are not coming, it becomes dry. Now nothing can change, either I will live or die, who cares? The dream I dreamt throughout my college life was fake and real life is too different.

Goodbye.

CHAPTER TWELVE

Unanswered Questions

Why is it so difficult to understand the other person in the current generation?

If Sakshi didn't want to come back, then why did she let me wait for her?

And even if she went, why didn't she answer all of my questions?

Does she know that she was wrong?

We had such deep love still we just separated without any official reason?

Suppose if we both were well settled in Pune or Mumbai doing our jobs and were independent, then would this break up have taken place just because her brother ordered?

Was this the result of a relationship in an immature age?

Since this relationship ended in such a way, will any new relationship can ever be called love?

Malav's letter

Hey Sakshi,

I loved you from all of my heart, I really loved you. It's okay if you have a past, it's okay if you were in a relationship with me, but then also you let another guy kiss you for 7 consecutive days. It's okay if your friend cum brother who entered your life after me (which I am sure, he won't be present in your life in future) and ordered you to stop talking with me and you just obeyed him forgetting our one and half year relationship of love'. That is also okay, since he stated that if your feelings are true, they will remain so forever. I waited for you for a year to prove that I have true feelings for you. But after all this sacrifice, what did I get as a result? Yes, I do respect you. Here I am just writing my feelings, maybe on the other side, you are also right. But still I feel if we have good communication skills such situations can be handled. Every relationship has some basic expectations, some basic respect. You don't even consider that I deserve a proper reason for ending our precious relationship. You just vanished from my life in a day and after a year you tell me that "Hum dil de chuke sanam". Seriously, is my life a Bollywood movie?

Do you have love feelings for someone else now?

Don't you have any feelings for me?

Was this just an attraction?

Should I die if I didn't get my love like many people commit suicide in love? I am depressed, I have fears, I have stress which results in breaking up of all other relations as well.

Such a long and important relationship has ended in this way? Does it feel right?

If it was a family reason, it might still be acceptable. But, seriously for no reason? It hurts more. It pinches in my heart. Believe me!

If I am thinking straight, when you stopped following your resolution for the first time, I felt its okay it is *just a message. Then slowly and gradually we reduced our chatting time from the whole day to just 2 hours and that too without any romance. The imagination on which you used to die once, you started to hate it. It is okay, you are a girl, I accepted all this with my heart. Mood swings or changes occur with time, it's okay I accepted all this. But how much more do I need to accept dear? Please let me prepare myself a little. Slowly and slowly the calls vanished, you forgot my schedule which I used to make according to you itself. It's okay, let me show maturity, I need to understand that you are at home. But I have a doubt, whenever I am unwell, I don't know from where you get guts that you show me so much love and care on that time in spite of being at home. I want that love forever so should I pray to God to make me sick forever? Can it be called selfishness? Why are you letting me die every moment? I know you are also feeling the same.*

I know you never intended to hurt me on Valentine day. I am so proud of your ability to speak the truth on such a day, but till it doesn't mean I don't get hurt at all. Whenever I'm feeling sad, I will remember all the things which hurt me by you or by us.

I really don't care what the world thinks of me even my close ones but your words, "I don't have feelings now" killed me and it's like someone close to me inserted a sharp knife inside me. You were taking all this out of your heart, but in real you are judging me that I was wrong. You could have helped me and corrected me, but you chose to leave me, 'It's okay, it's the harsh reality of the world. The truth is every relation has many unanswered questions.'

Malav

Author's Note

We finally finished reading the diary, Prakash and I looked towards each other. We both have tears in our eyes. Prakash wiped his tears and asked me, 'Do you have the answers to the unanswered questions?'

I said, 'I might have some of them. But it varies from person to person.'

I just want to conclude:

In the current generation, very easily kids get into relationships and it's not always love, I admit but it's also not always an attraction. Sometimes it's true love. But they need to learn if they can start their relationship at an improper age then at the same age they need to learn how to fight for their own love. I just ask one question to everyone who is married and settled. Answer me by keeping your hand to your heart, 'How many of you think that the reason at the age of 18 to 22 was the correct reason for the end of your relationship?'

To live your dreams is not the correct reason for breakup. To have differences is not the correct reason either. Putting in efforts is not wrong. Even in a marriage there is not a single couple who doesn't fight. *Learn to fight for your own love.* Don't give shove it off as an attraction due to your age or choices.

If you are in a relationship at your age and according to your wish, then you must know how to fight for it as well. *Be ready even if you want to fight with yourself.* You must find a way to keep that relation forever and you just need to accept that you can do that! Admit your own love, understand it, embrace it, give input, you will definitely get the output. I hope generations learn to stop breaking up with their partners in the name of practicality. Because, no matter what happens, the importance of love cannot be overshadowed. Love is always more important than every other thing: your job, work, choice, time, differences, etc. *Love is an unstoppable feeling.*

www.ingramcontent.com/pod-product-compliance
Ingram Content Group UK Ltd.
Pitfield, Milton Keynes, MK11 3LW, UK
UKHW022235230426
12048UKWH00018BA/1271

9 789354 275579